SO-AEF-736

THE
BAGGAGE
HANDLER

Center Point
Large Print

**This Large Print Book carries the
Seal of Approval of N.A.V.H.**

THE
BAGGAGE
HANDLER

a novel

DAVID RAWLINGS

CENTER POINT LARGE PRINT
THORNDIKE, MAINE

This Center Point Large Print edition
is published in the year 2019 by arrangement with
Thomas Nelson.

Lyrics for "You're Beautiful," performed by James Blunt, written by James Blunt, Sacha Skarbek, and Amanda Ghost.

The text of this Large Print edition is unabridged.
In other aspects, this book may vary
from the original edition.
Printed in the United States of America
on permanent paper.
Set in 16-point Times New Roman type.

ISBN: 978-1-64358-192-7

Library of Congress Cataloging-in-Publication Data

Names: Rawlings, David, 1971- author.
Title: The baggage handler / David Rawlings.
Description: Center Point Large print edition. | Thorndike, Maine :
   Center Point Large Print, 2019.
Identifiers: LCCN 2019006208 | ISBN 9781643581927 (hardcover :
   alk. paper)
Subjects: LCSH: Attitude (Psychology)—Fiction. |
   Change (Psychology)—Fiction. | Parables. | Psychological fiction. |
   Large type books.
Classification: LCC PR9619.4.R385 B34 2019b | DDC 823/.92—dc23
LC record available at https://lccn.loc.gov/2019006208

THE
BAGGAGE
HANDLER

What weighs us down is not our baggage but the decision to keep carrying it.

—1—

The sense of dread that began with Becky's email pressed Gillian Short deep into her seat as passengers filed past her down the aisle, a line of eye-rubbing yawns and bouncing impatience.

Gillian lifted the clasp on her still-tight seat belt. Her next moves should be simple: stand up, grab her carryall from the overhead bin, and start her trip. That's what everyone else was doing with ease.

But they weren't spending five days with her sister.

A young mother leaned across the aisle as she slid her sleeping infant into the sling across her chest. "Are you okay?"

Gillian adjusted her glasses and sighed. The answer bounced around inside her head. *No. I'd rather be anywhere but here.* But the words wouldn't come out. What sort of person wasn't excited about a family wedding?

Her.

The young mother slung a bag over her shoulder and grabbed the hand of her patient toddler.

Gillian's impolite silence filled the space where an answer should have gone. She changed the subject—a tried-and-true reflex.

9

"You have beautiful children. Do you need any help?"

"No, but thanks for offering. Have a great day." She grabbed a tiny backpack with her free hand and took her brood down the aisle.

Gillian shook her head in amazement. *I wish I was a mom like that.* When the boys were young, just wrangling them into high chairs seemed to require military precision and a week's worth of planning. Flying them anywhere would have been out of the question. Perhaps it was even now. Sure, the boys were older, but just thinking about the havoc they could wreak brought out a cold sweat.

The ratchet in her stomach clicked tighter.

Gillian pulled out her phone. Becky hadn't texted—yet. The siren song of Facebook, a song she could never deny, called to her. A flood of wonderful achievements flew past as she thumbed through holiday photos from afar and quotes designed to inspire her to greatness, ironic hashtags and political insights into how to fix a broken world, and photos of smiling families doing life together. The best of everyone. Facebook asked what was on her mind, a question she never answered with complete truth. *Had a great flight, now here for the wedding! Gonna have an amazing time!* The self-loathing washed over her the second her finger posted this sculpted thought into life.

The cabin was empty of people and full of stale air. She was stalling. Gillian sighed hard and stood.

Here goes.

After being summoned by her sister's email, she had made it. *You simply have to be here for your niece's wedding. Jessica is the first grandchild to marry, the whole family is coming, and goodness knows you haven't seen most of them in a while.*

It had been a whirlwind few days, organizing her husband so the boys could cope without Mom for three days and filling the freezer so they wouldn't starve.

She reached into the overhead bin for her large, floral carryall, and the ratchet in her stomach gripped her again. It had tightened the closer she got to her old hometown, and the turbulence hadn't helped. Some time away from the madhouse at home should have brought peace and some relief. Time to step outside an unrelenting schedule to catch up. Time to breathe. Time to enjoy the celebration and the closeness of family. But the whisper arose again in her ear. It had begun with Becky's email and persisted ever since.

You just need to get through it.

—2—

David Byrne sprinted to the heart of baggage claim, nestled under a web of steel spokes and polished metal. He skidded into a wall of bodies and chatter as five planes' worth of passengers crowded the baggage carousels.

David swore under his ragged breath. He wasn't in the mood for people getting in his way. Not after what happened last night.

He dodged through the crowd as he scanned each carousel for his flight number. Then, at the carousel farthest from the exit, the screen fizzed and crackled, and his flight number appeared above the static, black belt.

David swept away the beading sweat from his brow. He couldn't face the board as anything but cool. At least he'd have a chauffeured ride to the showdown meeting, his thoughts given clean air to run through the presentation that would show the board just how wrong they were. And the minibar would give him courage. He had given Sisyphus Financial his heart and soul for the last ten years. What more did they want?

His phone was silent. Nothing from Sharon. How could she misunderstand his ultimatum? *You need to promise me it's really over.*

Sharon was silent then and silent now.

David thumbed through his phone, looking for a text with the details for his arrival. His thumb came up empty. Twelve months ago the board had rolled out the red carpet: a limousine and a full minibar for the most profitable branch manager in the country. He winced. The last twelve months had been tough for business. They'd been tough for a lot of things.

His thumb hovered over a family photo from a happier time, the day Caitlin got her Elsa dress and his small family's obsession with *Frozen* began. Sharon was smiling—he could carbon-date the picture from that fact alone—but Caitlin was beaming. David's heart still seemed to swell when he thought of how happy he'd made his daughter that day. He'd hunted all over the city for the smallest dress size to turn his own princess into Disney royalty.

The more familiar hammer beat of stress took over as the reason for his trip shadowed across that happy thought from another time. If he lost his job, Caitlin's smile would fade. How could he let that happen to his six-year-old daughter?

A line of twelve suited men stood in the distance, their jaunty chauffeur's hats perched above a row of white cards held at their chests. *Which one is mine? Probably the big guy with the beaming white smile.*

The carousel, a winding, slumbering beast in black and silver, defied him. Behind the walls engines roared and tires squealed with the internal traffic of an airport. The other carousels were a hive of busyness too. Everyone but him got their suitcases and a release to start their day.

A throat politely cleared behind him. "Excuse me, sir?"

David glanced over his shoulder. A young man in a navy-blue cap and overalls leaned on a gleaming silver baggage cart. A white badge branded one breast: Baggage Services.

"Yes?"

The young man tipped his cap, and thick, black, curly hair threatened to burst free. He rose on the balls of his feet. "I'm the Baggage Handler. Do you need some help with your baggage?"

A stroke of luck. For the first time in a while.

David spun to face him. "Actually, buddy, I need to get out of here in a hurry, so if you could make my suitcase appear, that would be ideal."

The Baggage Handler smiled. "I'm afraid I can't make it appear, sir. But I am available to help you with your baggage when you're ready." His deep-blue eyes sparkled above a kind smile.

The nerves again launched a fresh assault on David. What was the holdup with his suitcase? He needed his sales reports to have any chance of keeping his job. Why couldn't the airline just do their job?

The Baggage Handler again rose on the balls of his feet. "The minute you want any help, you just let me know." He pushed his cart to the other end of the carousel.

What a strange guy.

The crowd swelled around him as the passengers from his flight meandered over, eroding his advantage and negating his sprint from the plane. David huffed and reached into his pocket for another antacid. The indigestion was getting worse, an obvious symptom of fighting to save his future and preparing to justify his existence before a board of twelve uninterested men whose concern for him stopped at his ability to make them money.

At least that was David's self-diagnosis of indigestion, with the help of Dr. Google.

A woman sidled next to him and, sweating, hefted a large, floral carryall over her shoulder. She looked like she wanted to be anywhere but there. A kindred spirit.

David leaned across to her. "A good flight?"

The woman replied only with a pasted smile to shut down the conversation. David was used to that smile. Sharon had perfected it in the past few months.

The carousel shuddered once, and David swung back to the gaps in the heavy rubber flaps. Vague shapes moved between them, and the sound of brakes slipped out, a curling finger of enticement to his impatience.

The carousel moved at an arthritic, glacial

speed. A baggage sticker—stuck to the belt for all eternity—moved past him on a mesmerizing crawl and bent around a corner out of sight. Still his baggage remained a prisoner in the bowels of the airport.

Come on!

Gillian's phone beeped with a text, and in an instant she became an observer in her own life.

I'm walking in. Will be there in a minute to carry your bag.

Becky, always the protective older sister. A superhero who loved the cape.

A squeal burst over her shoulder, and she turned to see a young woman throw herself into the arms of a young man carrying a huge bouquet.

I wish Rick would meet me like that.

Her phone rang in her hand, and Becky's voice somehow sounded in her ear before she even answered the call. "Gilly, I'm at baggage claim. Where are you?"

Her big sister teetered on her tiptoes three carousels away, searching the crowded baggage area. Then she waved in recognition and rushed over, shoving her way through the throng.

"I'm so happy you made it." Becky held Gillian by the shoulders. "Let me see you."

Gillian didn't want to be seen. Her gaze hit the floor as she once again stood in the shadow of her sister—a tall frame wrapped in a pencil dress, perfection from styled blond hair to painted toenails poking through Dolce & Gabbana open-toed shoes. She squirmed under the inspection, acutely aware of hair that was the victim of a predawn start, makeup still in her suitcase, and under her eyes, bags that wouldn't have been out of place on the carousel.

"How are you?" Becky enveloped Gillian in a powerful hug. "A silly question to ask. I know you had a great flight. I've got to drop off my designs for the floral arrangements for our rehearsal dinner, so I'll drop you home and then do that. I've booked Marcellinas for lunch so we can catch up. It's been awhile. Anyway, much turbulence? You got to the airport okay?"

As always, Becky jumped from topic to topic like a *Jeopardy* contestant on an espresso bender. She disengaged with a jolt.

"Anyway, it's terrific to have you here. I'm so thrilled you could come. It's been too long, and it will be a great week, and we're all so excited about Jessica's wedding. She *is* the first grandchild to get married."

So it began. Five days of Becky not only gushing like a fire hose about her life, but also about how much better she was at life than Gillian was.

"Where's your bag, then?" Becky looked over the heads crowding the carousel. Through a heady waft of Chanel, Gillian focused on a hot-pink button on Becky's shoulder, which was at Gillian's eye level: "Mother of the Bride. This is my day too."

Her big sister elbowed her way through the crowd, shoving aside a young man in a hoodie, and then perching, vulture-like, over the carousel.

It was going to be a long few days.

Michael Downer picked himself up from the cold, buffed floor as his stomach, ignored on a morning flight that required a small loan to buy air-dried fresh sandwiches or ten-dollar breakfast bars, rumbled. His father had paid for this flight and given him cab fare to and from the university, plus thirty dollars to buy a Clarendon University sweatshirt so he could impress the coach. But nothing more.

The trip was the next step in a plan for Michael's life that he had no say in. Yet this was his single chance for college—an opportunity for a track scholarship at Clarendon University and the reason he'd flown in a hoodie and track pants rather than in his more comfortable jeans and cherished Jackson Pollock T-shirt. But the scholarship would keep open a door to his dream of studying art, the only way he could keep his dream alive and his father happy. Two uncomfortable bedfellows.

Michael's body and spirit had been created in two different workshops. His seventeen-year-old lithe frame was built for running, but his spirit soared with sketching pencils in hand. Yet his father saw only one side of him, and that was why he was here to meet the great Coach Crosswell. A track scholarship was part of the plan to become an Olympian and "make it." Whatever that meant.

He didn't know what was worse—getting a scholarship that would push him down a path he didn't want or missing out and getting a life sentence working in hardware. The latter would mean downshifting his passion to a hobby and selling it for next to nothing on eBay, in between shifts of stocking shelves with things he cared little about. A "real" job. Soul-dissolving, but "real." And with his father as a boss.

Still, this was his best—maybe only—chance. If he could get the track scholarship, art could become his major. That was the only way to shoehorn his artistic dream into his father's vision of sporting glory. He was sure he wouldn't be good enough for an art scholarship, despite the confidence of his art teachers.

Michael, you're a talented artist. You need to believe in yourself.

Michael, you were born with a special gift, and your best will be more than good enough.

But the ever-present thought lurking in the shadows of his mind lurched forward and gripped him. *No, it won't be. My best won't be good enough.*

Michael batted it away, but it left its numbing residue on him as it had for years.

There was no escaping it; his father would never approve his studying art, which would lead, in his words, nowhere.

He had one chance.

The road to being an artist ran through Coach Crosswell at Clarendon University. He would meet the man whose name his father dropped almost constantly and run a great time to impress him. And then he would sneak away from the track to see the art school. His art teacher had emailed some samples to a friend—who also happened to be an associate art professor at Clarendon—and encouraged Michael to drop in. The school was just behind the athletics facilities anyway.

One chance.

3

The carousel creaked on. Still empty.

Three chauffeur-hatted drivers remained at the terminal exit. One *had* to be for David; he just couldn't read the cards from his place at the carousel.

The stuck baggage sticker snuck out from under the heavy rubber flap and greeted him on its second agonizingly slow lap.

Stress caught his chest in its viselike grip. His heart pounded inside its restrictive cage, a now-familiar lilting, unbalanced cadence. His ears rang and his jaw clenched, as it was doing more and more. He reached for another antacid.

The heavy rubber flaps of the carousel lifted, and a black suitcase peeked out and leaped forward into the spotlight.

Finally.

David rubbed his hands together and leaned across the suitcase. Gold frequent flyer baggage tags, not his proud red alumni livery. He cursed under his breath.

A second bag emerged and then a third. Each was black. Each badged as a priority. Neither belonged to David. The knots in his jaw flexed as he ground his teeth.

Suitcases emerged into the light. Black, black,

black, gray, black, black, silver. David could feel his blood pressure sizzle and spit as each one passed. The baggage sticker started its third lap. Stuck to the carousel. Just like him.

A familiar black suitcase with a flash of red around the handle pried apart the carousel's heavy flaps. David scanned the terrain as he swung the suitcase from the carousel. More planes had emptied their passengers into baggage claim, and his path to the exit was now blocked.

He plowed his way through the throng. Only one suited driver was left. *That has to be my guy.*

David thumbed through his phone again as he charged through the crowd. Still nothing from Sharon. How hard was it to promise it was over? The evidence on her phone flashed red in his memory. His cheeks flushed—

Crash.

David had tripped over an empty baggage cart. As his suitcase skidded across the polished floor, he staggered, arms windmilling, into a tour group. Their guide broke his fall, which started a round of staccato jabbering in some foreign language. Pain shot through his shin, and David added some choice adjectives from his own language as he picked himself up and brushed off his suit. The tour group stood back, their phones raised to capture their first taste of this new culture.

The same young man in the Baggage Services uniform offered a simple smile. "I'm so sorry, sir." He tipped his cap, and black, curly hair threatened to spring free. "We all should watch where we're heading. May I help with your baggage?"

David rubbed his throbbing shin and growled through clenched teeth. "You can help me by staying out of my way."

The young man reversed his cart with a flourish. "Happy to help in any way I can, sir!"

David muttered under his breath about everything—and nothing. As he approached the exit, he lowered his shoulder to barge his way through the crowd, again ignoring protests against his charge. The name printed on the card of the remaining driver was now clear: Professor Ivor Wachokowsky. David's chest thumped along on its unsteady drumbeat as he calculated his next move—a cheeky thought. He could be a professor for twenty minutes, just enough time to get out of the airport as fast as possible. He could tackle the case of mistaken identity closer to the city and his meeting. He affixed his brightest smile and beelined for the driver, who returned the smile before he resumed his visual search over David's shoulder.

It wasn't going to work.

David strode through the double doors of the terminal and into a thick curtain of humidity and heat. Long lines snaked their way toward the taxi stands. He reached for yet another antacid, his stomach churning and his mind ablaze. Sweat trickled down his back under his shirt and pooled at his belt line. If the cab's air-conditioning wasn't working, the ride would make the melting worse. Much worse. The limousine ride was supposed to help him arrive cool and collected. Nothing screamed desperation during a corporate presentation like someone sweating bullets.

Why was there no car?

Another dozen black bags dawdled past as Gillian tottered on tiptoes. A light-blue bag sailed by, defiant in its individuality. *I wish I'd bought blue instead of black.*

Becky shouted over her shoulder from her hard-won place at the carousel. "What color is your bag, Gilly?"

"Black."

"Of course. Only about a thousand black bags are coming off your plane." Becky's hand-on-hip pose threw Gillian back to years of childhood lectures about dolls or boys . . . or breathing. "That's why I always travel with my pink luggage. You should think about getting some."

Gillian breathed deep. Guilt about not coming to see her sister had dripped into her emotional tank for two years, but the past five minutes had pulled the plug.

"May I help with your baggage?" Gillian

jumped at the voice that appeared at her shoulder. A young man in a navy-blue Baggage Services cap smiled at her.

"My sister's getting it at the moment." Gillian couldn't help but smile at the gesture. "But thanks for asking."

"If you need help with your baggage, just let me know." The young man tipped his cap, black, curly hair springing free. He spun his cart and melted back into the crowd.

Becky bellowed over her shoulder. "How will I know which one is yours?"

"Red baggage tags." Gillian's voice bounced back to her from the emptying claim area.

"I've got frequent flyer tags that make a huge difference. They saved me about an hour when we went to Maui."

Gillian's phone beeped. A text from Rick. A chance to drop out of her sister's orbit for a moment. *Hi, gorgeous. Hope you had a good flight. The boys all got off to school okay, although James lost his gym bag. By now you'll have had your ear chewed off by Becky. Lucky you've got two! Bail you out when we arrive. R xx.*

"I've got it!" Becky swung a black suitcase from the carousel and almost decapitated a young boy sitting next to his tiny backpack. She charged past Gillian, her phone stuck to her ear as she squeezed through the crowd toward the exit. "Come on. I've got to get my designs to the florist."

Gillian fell in behind her sister, eight years old again. And, like in her childhood, it wasn't long before Becky's long legs left Gillian behind. She pushed her glasses back up on the bridge of her nose and sped up as fast as her short legs would carry her. She dodged carts—and children who were escaping their parents' clutches to make a break for freedom. A flash caught her eye; an animated billboard drooled over the latest Audi and promised the same reaction from Gillian's friends if it were parked in her driveway. *As if that would ever happen.*

Becky swung around and walked backward. "Hurry, Gilly!" she barked, and then she turned around to again charge away, her long gait cutting a swathe through the crowd.

Gillian hefted her carryall onto her shoulder. Becky was almost at the exit, and Gillian raced after her, the old thoughts returning like unwelcome housemates. *If only I had legs like hers.*

A gap at the carousel opened for Michael as the crowd thinned.

A light-blue suitcase sailed past him in a sea of black baggage. Another anxious thought jumped unbidden into his mind—the curse of any traveler enduring the agonizing wait at an airport carousel. *I hope my suitcase arrives.* He couldn't prove his athletic wares without his running spikes, and he couldn't impress the faculty at the art school without his drawings.

Michael had emerged from Dad's car at the airport with the obligatory micromanaging lecture ringing in his ears: *carry your training gear with you just in case.* His seventeen years had taught him arguing with his father was pointless, so he had perfected the interested nod while mentally stepping away.

The light-blue bag began a third lap of the carousel. Still no sign of Dad's red baggage tags.

As he had watched his father drive away, the slightest rebellion swelled within him, and he put his running spikes in his suitcase before checking it. But now, as the wait stretched, that rebellion cast a long shadow over him, and the point he wanted to make pecked at his already frayed nerves. If his suitcase was lost, even for a while, he would miss out on the scholarship and once again hear about how he didn't measure up. But worse, he'd lose his design portfolio forever if his suitcase were permanently lost. Why hadn't he carried it with him?

A black suitcase with a flash of red around the handle twisted and danced as it entered the belt. Thank goodness for that. Michael checked his phone. He still had time to get a cab and have a few minutes up his sleeve before the interview with Coach Crosswell. He excused his way through the thinning throng as he edged along the carousel toward his suitcase.

The whirs and chirps of R2-D2 burst from his phone. A text. Dad. *I've checked Google Maps, and you should have a good run to the university. Traffic looks good.*

Michael toyed with the need to respond and settled on the path of least resistance. With a sigh, he thumbed his reply—*thanks*—and then slung the suitcase off the carousel.

A young man in navy-blue overalls and cap emblazoned with a Baggage Services logo appeared in front of him. "Morning, sir. Would you like help with your baggage?"

Michael looked over first one shoulder and then the other. *Sir? Who is this guy talking to?* Oh well, it would be a shame not to take advantage of a fleeting feeling of importance.

"That would be great. I'll take a cart if you have one."

The young man stood aside to reveal a shiny silver cart. "It's all yours, sir." He hefted Michael's suitcase onto the cart with effortless ease and spun it toward the exit. He bowed with a smile. "I've been dealing with baggage for many years."

Years? This guy looked thirty. If that.

"Where can I get a cab?"

The young man pointed to the far end of the terminal.

"Thanks for your help." Michael pushed the cart toward the wall of people outside the door, but it had other ideas. One of its four wheels was now keen to explore its own path, and Michael leaned hard to keep the cart heading toward the taxis, throwing apologies left and right as his erratic charge ran into the backs of legs and small children.

The doors slid open, and Michael walked into an oven. He joined the back of a taxi queue full of sweaty, impatient travelers inching their way forward. R2-D2 whistled again in his pocket and he wrestled out his phone.

Dad.

Again.

I've uploaded footage of your last five races and emailed Coach Crosswell. Don't forget to mention it, Mikey.

Mikey—a name he'd outgrown long ago but his father insisted on using, keeping him tethered at eight years of age. Michael inched forward in the heat. No "Good luck." No best wishes. Just more orders.

Another buzz. Michael wrestled with the idea of ignoring it but again knew it wasn't worth it.

Remember: the future belongs to those who believe in their dreams.

If he had a dollar for every time he'd heard that

from Dad while he was growing up, he could buy his own art gallery. A sly question slunk its way into his mind, a question he resented more and more.

What if the dream isn't yours?

4

David corralled his nerves and forced them into one knee, which bounced an erratic dance as he sat in the reception area of Sisyphus Financial's top floor. He wriggled his shoulders to unstick the shirt from his back and wiped his brow with a damp handkerchief.

Why was there no car?

On his last trip, the company president had welcomed him, the company's rising star, with open arms into his office for brunch and champagne. This time he'd received a polite but firm request from the receptionist to wait to be called, and she was doing everything she could to not look at him. His knee hammered away as the sweat dripped down his back and seeped into his suit. His body screamed at him to remove his jacket so it could access the cool crispness of the corporate air-conditioning, but the circles under his arms wouldn't help him paint the calm and confident picture he needed.

Why was there no car?

Above David's head, a TV screen pumped out 24/7 business news. "And in this ever-competitive market, unemployment numbers are up again by another 2 percent, which could spell devastating losses and provoke carnage across job markets." The reporter delivered this serious pronouncement on the economy as if beaming in live from a war zone. "But it will increase corporate profits by at least 15 percent, so improved dividends for shareholders will be welcome news."

He couldn't lose his job. He'd slugged out eighteen-hour days for months to keep it, to keep his family happy. Sure, he hadn't been around much, but he had to provide for them. The voices that complained he was never around were the same ones asking for better furniture, better clothes, better toys . . .

The nerves escaped David's knee, and he fidgeted on a squeaky leather couch lubricated by his telltale sweat. He again ran through the introduction to the pitch that would save his career. He breathed deep in a desperate attempt to force away the tension.

Julian Sporne, the regional director and David's boss, stepped into the reception area with an extended hand. His crisp Armani shamed David's creased and damp off-the-rack suit. "Morning, David. A good flight up?"

David? What happened to Dave? David's stomach lurched at the more formal greeting his boss offered. "Okay. I've done it enough times, as you know. Bit bumpy on the way down. New suit?"

No familiarity showed in Julian's eyes, and he

offered none of the usual banter—just a stiffness, a distance from a guy who had hit the town as hard as David on each visit. David stared hard at him, analyzing him to find a reason.

Julian wiped the greasiness from David's handshake onto his pants. "You're sweating a bit. Nervous?" Then he displayed a stone-faced expression, and another pause, pregnant with unasked questions and answers not volunteered, sat between them.

David shot another look at the receptionist, who turned away. "Look, call me paranoid, but last time there was a car waiting for me at the airport. Not today."

Julian flicked a glance at the receptionist, who stared at her screen with even more intensity.

Uh-oh.

Julian looked over David's shoulder at the stock market coverage on the TV. David moved his head into Julian's eyeline. "Should I read anything into that?"

"Let's head into my office so you can get ready for your presentation." Julian stepped back and held open the glass door as he gestured David through.

David's mind raced as he dragged his black suitcase toward Julian's office. But Julian kept walking down the corridor, and David flung open Julian's office door to an unfamiliar face.

"Hey!" A young woman in a serious corporate

power suit looked up from where Julian's desk once stood. "May I help you?"

Julian clamped a hand on David's shoulder. "They've moved my office. I'm in the corner suite now. This way."

David followed Julian, this new development opening an escape hatch. Corner suite? A promotion for his boss was a *good* sign. The whole division must be doing well. Comfort settled over his anxiety like a fluffed quilt falling onto a bed.

He stepped into Julian's office and whistled as he took in the 90-degree view of the city, framed by huge windows. Rich leather furniture grazed under a collection of sports memorabilia plastered across one wall. To his right, a bittersweet aroma drifted across from a gleaming coffee machine.

The young woman in the corporate power suit poked her head through the doorway. "They'll be ready for the first presentation in twenty minutes, Mr. Sporne." He nodded.

As Julian sat down behind his desk, David eased into a leather guest chair and took in the scope of his boss's new corporate digs. The tension in his shoulders eased and the sweat on his brow evaporated in the crisp air. He sat back, his hands laced behind his head. "This is great! I thought I was coming here to justify why my branch shouldn't be closed. If you've got a new corner suite, our division must be flying."

Julian steepled his fingers under his nose and took a moment before responding. "Yes, about that . . ."

David stretched and rubbed his hands together. "This is great to see. While this year wasn't our best, once the board sees some of the new initiatives I've got planned for next year—"

"They're not keen on new initiatives." Julian stared over his fingertips at David, his voice an almost sinister monotone. "They're keen on seeing why you should continue the current ones."

Continue? David tried a well-practiced approach with a proven track record. "Come on, Jules. We're friends, aren't we? How long have we known each other? Ten years?"

If flattery was art, David was Picasso. But today Julian was no art lover. He nodded, his eyes like cold, dead fish.

"And we've had some great nights out on the town." David chuckled at the memory. "Do you remember the last trip six months ago? When we went to that bar—"

Julian leaned forward on his elbows, now boss and not fellow drinker. "You've got to understand these decisions today aren't being made around length of friendships. We've got to streamline our business to squeeze out some extra profits. What you need to do is provide some financials that show why we should keep your branch open."

One word snagged in David's mind. *We.* He snatched at other options as the flattery—which always worked, always—fell flat, and Julian removed his trump card from the table.

"David, I need to close ten branches across the country."

David lurched forward and gripped the arms of the chair. "Ten branches?"

"I need to meet an expenses reduction target of 15 percent, so I need to cut back—"

"Cut back?" David flushed and waved his hand around the room, his voice rising a notch. "Does closing ten branches cover the cost of your new office? The sports memorabilia? The coffee machine? How many branches is all that worth?"

Julian didn't rise to the bait. "There's no need to be like that. You've got forty-five minutes to convince us your branch shouldn't be one of those ten. If your presentation is good, you'll survive. You have the same chance as the other branch managers presenting today."

Us.

The distance Julian put between them yawned into a gaping silence. David jumped one step ahead and calculated his options, as he always did. "How many presentations are there today?"

"Twelve. You're the first."

The sweat reappeared on his brow as David's stomach lurched again. Two out of twelve were not good odds. But his defiant confidence muscled that sinking feeling out of the way. "Okay, I'll take two out of twelve. No other manager will knock the socks off the board like I will. Thanks for putting me first, by the way. I'll set a standard no one else will meet." He reached for the suitcase. "Let me show you what I've prepared."

As he unzipped the suitcase, the flash of red was familiar and yet somehow not. He flung open the lid, but he didn't see his printed financials and his casuals for hitting the town with Julian that night. Instead, a woman's dress and some kind of warped and distorted hand mirror sat in what he now knew was someone else's suitcase, along with a smattering of photos of a happy family.

David swore under his breath. This baggage wasn't his.

—5—

Michael rounded the bend in the hallowed Clarendon University running track, his calves twitching for action, unused to this slow pace. Usually he would lean hard into the curve, not dawdle behind a middle-aged man dressed in the obligatory cap, oversize shorts, and whistle hanging over a burgeoning paunch. A track coach who held the key to his dream of being an artist.

Coach Crosswell turned to him. "Your dad tells me you live for the track." He had an abrasive voice, roughened after years of instructions shouted, never spoken.

Michael thrust his hands deep into his track pants pockets. "Honestly, Coach, the track is what I was made for." That did sound good, even if it was only half true.

Coach nodded. "That's exactly what I want to hear, Michael, although your dad said you prefer to be called Mikey."

Michael clenched fistfuls of pocket as his father pulled another string in his life. "I'd prefer Michael, Coach."

"No problem. You're a lot taller than him, you know—or at least what I remember from our days at Serviceton High School. And I hope you're a heck of a lot faster."

Michael nearly chuckled. His father had never even tried athletics.

Coach quickened his pace, head down, and resumed his graveled sales pitch to the two-toned blue track. "We have a great athletic history here at old CU—Olympians, national championships—a great legacy to the noble pursuit of track and field. We're so proud of our forty-million-dollar athletic center . . ."

Michael's eyes wandered over the empty rows of steel and concrete in the grandstand and floated to the south of the campus, where his future lay—at the art school.

"Michael!"

The graveled half shout wrenched Michael back to the track. Coach Crosswell eyed him with suspicion. "You've come a long way to see our facilities here, and I'm doing your father a huge favor, but it looks like your mind is elsewhere, young man. Normally I wouldn't give anyone this type of personal once-over, but your dad and I did go to school together."

Michael flushed, sure his face had turned a beet red. He couldn't lose this opportunity, and his mouth scrambled to answer a question his ears had missed. "It's just so much to take in—the history, the fact so many great athletes have been a part of your program here."

Coach smiled. "Well, that's true. And if you have the privilege of being selected to come here,

39

you can join them. We'll make you into the best version of you possible." He laced his fingers behind his back and resumed his strut down the homestretch. Michael fell in behind him, mentally kicking himself.

"Imagine when you're tearing down the straight to claim another four-hundred-meter win. This will be full of people cheering your name—what every athlete dreams of."

Michael looked up to the empty stands and nodded, his mind pulling on a tight leash as it strove to fast-forward to the art school visit.

Coach's eyes narrowed, and his pace slowed. "Next stop will be the athletic center—just a great facility for our athletes." He stopped and looked at his feet. "But this is home."

Michael looked down at the line painted across the track, a line with which he was very familiar.

Coach Crosswell swept his hand across the expanse of the grandstand's front row. "This section is reserved for family. As you cross the line, your dad will be here to celebrate your great wins."

Michael nodded. At least that was one time when he and his father had a connection.

The coach thrust his hands into the pockets of his shorts. "You will come to love this line because it will be your goal every day until you graduate."

Michael toed the line with his shoe. This was the price he had to pay.

Coach Crosswell's hard breathing snapped him back to the present. He looked down into eyes that were almost scanning Michael, sizing him up.

"Son, your dad has been emailing me for months, telling me you're an athletic superstar and begging me for this visit. I've seen your results, and you've got potential, but you don't strike me as the sort of kid who lives for the track."

Art school was slipping through his fingers. Michael tried to inflate the enthusiasm clearly leaking out of him. "I'll be here every morning for training, Coach."

Coach Crosswell cocked his head and laid a fatherly hand on Michael's shoulder. "Son, do you really want to be here? Hundreds will be applying for this scholarship."

Under the squeeze of Coach's hand, a part of Michael wanted to tear down the wall he had crafted around a dream that was never acknowledged, around an artist's heart that was shunned. He wanted to shout to the empty stands that he didn't want to be here. He just wanted his pencils in hand.

But honesty led to hardware.

He reached for his tried-and-true pasted smile, the same expression that fended off his father's enthusiastic questions when he'd skipped another training session and instead gone to the high school art studio—his real home.

Michael scuffed at the finish line. "I *am* very excited, and I'm sorry if I'm not showing you that. It's just overwhelming. I do want to be here at Clarendon University."

Coach gave a knowing smile.

"And please excuse my father. He's just over-excited about the opportunity."

Coach Crosswell chuckled as he turned and left the track, striding toward the gym. "I've met all sorts of parents, Michael—the quiet, proud ones, and the pushy, overbearing ones like your dad. May I give you some advice?"

Michael strained to hear what the coach had to say. It was a nice change to be asked if he minded before advice was thrown at him. "Sure."

"Most of those pushy parents are pushing their kids into a dream that's actually theirs."

Something within Michael pawed to get out, but the hardware shelves beckoned. He swallowed the rising anxiety as he fell in line behind the man who held the pass to his future. He was making a mess of this; the best thing would be to head to the track and show the coach why he would be worthy of a scholarship.

Coach Crosswell held open the gym door. "Your father has sent me countless videos of you on the track, but I'd love to see you run for myself. Let's get you into some spikes. Where's your bag?"

They squeaked their way across a basketball court. "I think I left it in your office." But the artist within him had one more question. "When it comes to studying, how much time will I have to fit in track?"

The coach ushered him into an office lined from floor to ceiling with paper—graphs of achievement, charts of improvement, and schedules that ran students' lives. "Michael, I want my athletes giving 110 percent. I think you'll find it's more about how much time you'll have to fit in your studies." Coach stood back, arms folded. "Grab your spikes, and let's see what you've got."

A black suitcase sat next to a neat stack of traffic cones. Michael laid it down and squatted next to it. That's when he realized the flash of red he'd seen on the carousel wasn't from his father's cherished baggage tags. Instead, he saw the red of a university sporting team. The Rams, or something like that. And the barcode didn't display his name.

Oh no.

Coach laughed. "Well, if you do make it here, we'll have to get you the royal blue of Clarendon U!"

Michael's hand dropped, and he stared at the suitcase.

Coach leaned in. "Is there a problem?"

Michael's mind already answered a question it wasn't game enough to ask. "I've got the wrong suitcase."

"Didn't you check it when you picked it up at the airport?"

Michael gave a heavy sigh as his art dream shimmered and threatened to evaporate. The heaviness in the pit of his stomach seemed to sink into his feet and then into the floor as he put his head into his hands. "I can't run without my spikes."

The coach placed a meaty hand on Michael's shoulder. "I can try to rustle up some from around here. You can run in those."

But Michael's loss was greater than that. His design portfolio was gone. "I can't do this without my stuff." Tears bubbled just below the thin veneer of his confidence.

"Okay. Call the airline. I'll still look for some spikes here."

Michael sucked in a deep breath and whipped out his phone as the coach left the room. He Googled the airline's number, and his call was put through to Baggage Services. The airline's on-hold music—its latest cheesy advertisement that claimed to value its customers more than its share price—was cut off by a click and a whir and a chirpy, young male voice. "Thank you for calling Baggage Services."

"Um, I've got the wrong suitcase from my flight—"

"I'm sorry to hear that. We'll arrange for your baggage to be at our city depot inside the hour. Please bring the baggage you've got." He gave Michael the address.

The coach swung around the doorframe, his whistle banging into the woodwork. "We don't have any extra spikes around here. You're going to have to find your suitcase."

Michael stood up in a rush. "I need to get to this address in some place called the Docklands."

"That's about ten minutes away, although I didn't think there was much over there. I tell you what, son. I can book you a cab, but the university can't pay for it. If I could take you myself, I would."

Michael nodded as he fought the anxiety that rose again. He had to get his design portfolio back. "How much will it cost me to get there?"

"Ten, twelve bucks?"

That was okay. He'd have enough money for all his cab rides, and a few extra shifts of dishwashing at his job at the restaurant would pay for the sweatshirt he could probably order online. He'd nod through the expected verbal spray.

"I need you back here as quickly as possible.

This is a favor for your dad, and I've got wall-to-wall meetings after the time I've set aside for you."

He had to hurry back.

—6—

Gillian sat in silence as a perfect neighborhood scrolled past her car window. Model houses. Manicured gardens. Flower beds and blades of grass sculpted into place. A picture of her own garden, weeds and all, skulked around the edges of her memory.

Becky *had* to have a new car to go along with the new house. "Well, it just made sense to upgrade the old rust bucket we were driving. It was the oldest one at the tennis club there for a while." A "rust bucket" ten years newer than Gillian's.

The expensive leather of the car seat squeaked as a blast of icy air from the Audi's brand-new air-conditioning system caressed Gillian's cheek. She stared out the window as a better life than hers flashed past in the shimmering heat.

Becky tapped her leather driving gloves on the steering wheel. "You seem quiet. Is everything okay?"

"Just tired, I guess."

Gillian's evasion fired a starting pistol for Becky's next breathless self-pronouncement. "My new relaxation regime is what you need. It's all the benefits of yoga and tai chi with some kickboxing thrown in. I haven't had this much energy in years. Mind you, I've needed it considering we've just moved into the house and I've had to organize all the interior decorating and gardens and you're never quite sure if you're going to be able to keep up with all the maintenance . . ."

Becky's voice bounced around the inside of Gillian's head until her mind could catch up with all the updates crammed into one rapid-fire verbal attack.

"If your house is anything like these, I'm sure it's amazing."

Becky brushed off the compliment. "It's not much, but you do what you can with the money you have, don't you?"

No statement was ever more true.

"Anyway, is Rick okay? The boys okay? They're still joining us for the wedding, aren't they?"

Gillian was relieved when her sister opened a door for her to share about her life. "Yes, they're coming. Rick is driving up with the boys on Friday. He can't get any more time off work with the way his business is going." She reeled in the rest of her answer to leave an opening for her sister to take an interest in her, to ask a question giving her the chance to offload the pressure of Rick's job and the strain on the family.

"Good. It wouldn't be a full family picture for the wedding album if they weren't here." Becky slammed the opening shut. "Anyway, your being here alone gives us girls the chance to catch up."

"Of course." *I thought we were.* "You seem run off your feet with all these arrangements. How is Brent doing?"

Becky pursed her lips as she pulled out of an answer. "We're here."

Tires squealed on the flagstones as she swung her Audi into the horseshoe driveway, which led to a three-story house, shining with new paint. It could have been the centerfold for a home-decorating magazine. Perfect white shutters, fringed with a hint of white lace, stood against a dark-gray backdrop. Gables framed in cream and white pointed to the sky while set against a slated roof, weathered to perfection. At the top of slate steps, two white columns seated on pebble-stone plinths flanked a front door in rich oak.

"So this is home for the next few days." Becky charged up the steps and into the house, pulling Gillian's suitcase. A connection between sisters evaporated in an instant.

Gillian stood next to the car and, open-mouthed, took in the majesty of her sister's home. That gnawing feeling skulking in the shadows leaped forward and mugged her. Rick often joked that Gillian would compare herself with anyone who walked past, but this was sensory overload to her self-esteem. She hadn't even ventured inside yet. And it belonged to her sister.

With a deep breath to steel herself, she ascended the slate steps and entered her sister's perfect life.

The foyer took her breath away. Polished floorboards ran from under her feet through to a living room, which was a decor lesson in sharp edges and contrast. Rich leather furniture settled into comfort alongside glass-and-steel coffee tables. Beyond the furniture, a double staircase wound its way to the upper floor and even more living space. To one side, an oversized coach light hanging from the high ceiling presided over the dining room. A long, majestic dark-oak table split the space, attended by twelve leather dining chairs.

Gillian's head swam as she scrambled for a suitable response, but it was hard to take it all in. "Wow."

Becky buzzed past her, phone in hand, headed for the staircase. "Sorry about the mess, but, you know, I have spent all my time arranging the wedding, and life is just frantic!"

The mess? Accent pillows were strategically placed and yet thrown with a casual indifference onto the sofas. It was so far from Gillian's own living room, where items weren't placed; they just stayed where they landed.

Gillian had taken in only half of the house on this floor. To her right was a massive home theater, an entire wall plastered with a black screen, itself backlit with cinematic lighting. Recliner chairs were arranged in a basic worship pattern around it, and a popcorn machine offered its services from a stand next to the wall. *A popcorn machine?*

Becky bounced down the stairs and flashed past her again, a sheath of papers in hand, firing conversation topics like a ninja wielding death stars. "As you can see, we simply had to buy all new furniture. There was no way our old furniture would fit. I was planning to hold the wedding out back, but I decided the garden wasn't ready. I'll hold all our pre-wedding events there instead. If you want to grab some water, the kitchen's just past the dining nook."

The kitchen was a spotless tribute to reflection and polish. Even the cat's litter box was immaculate, raked like a Japanese garden. Gillian put her carryall on the large marble island bench and was drawn to a sweeping wall display—a showcase of photographs, cradled in gold frames, the chronology of a happy life. Proud Becky with her newborn. Becky and Jessica smiling in the snow. Becky and Jessica both dressed as ballerinas. Becky with Jessica in graduation gown and cap. Brent and Jessica holding a gleaming softball trophy. Perfect smiles beamed at her from every frame.

Gillian's photographs were stuck at random angles to her fridge, the constant gathering point for the four ravenous men in her life. They were family moments captured in time, complete with blinks, frowns, and more often than not, rabbit ears lurking behind an unsuspecting victim's head.

Becky sprinted past Gillian toward the front door, throwing her last words over her shoulder. "I've put your suitcase in one of the guest bedrooms upstairs. Make yourself at home. I won't be long, so be ready, because we need to be at Marcellinas for lunch in twenty minutes." And with that, she slammed the door behind her, the echo finding its way into the kitchen.

Gillian was now alone in this monolith of a house, home to just three people. Her mind swirled out of control, and her self-loathing rose up in her like floodwater. She needed to touch base with something tangible, so she texted Rick. *Made it to Becky's. This place is incredible. We're heading off to lunch next. I hope you have a good day at work.*

She wandered the second floor, looking for the right guest bedroom. Each room she peeked into was a window into perfection. The billiard room, with the half-moon walnut minibar presiding over it. Her brother-in-law Brent's study, his sports trophies lining one wall, his guitars framed on another. Another five minutes of searching and she found her suitcase on a king-sized bed in a guest bedroom bigger than her own. Through the windows, she could see a team of workmen assembling a white marquee on the back lawn.

Her phone beeped again. Rick. *Glad to hear you've made it. Look forward to seeing the house. I know it will be hard for you, but we love you. Will check in tonight when the boys are home and after I've fixed the starter on the car.* That darn car. A mechanic's retirement plan on wheels.

An almost primal need struck Gillian—to improve herself, to dress up to the standard of this colossal house. She was so out of place in this perfect life. The whisper started again. She was used to its constant hints of her inadequacy, but the whisper grew into a roar.

Gillian unzipped the bag, and a flash of gold set off a subconscious warning that made her furrow her brow. Instead of her blue dress—the one Rick had insisted she wear to the wedding reception— the suitcase was full of men's clothes, along with what looked like school certificates and a sports trophy. She checked the baggage tags on the handle, her brain already answering the next unasked question. While the baggage tags were red, they weren't from her travel agent.

I wish I'd picked up my own suitcase.

The front door slammed. "Let's go, Gilly!"

Gillian stood on the horns of a dilemma. *I have to get back to the airport.* She looked down at her creased blouse and dress pants, damp from sweat. She sighed as she lowered the lid on someone else's baggage. She'd need to go back to the airport and sort out the mess her sister had created. She padded down the stairs. "Becky, I've got the wrong suitcase."

Becky raced past her, her head down. "Mmm?"

Gillian sighed again as she reached the foot of the staircase. She tried one more time. "When you grabbed my baggage at the airport, did you check the baggage tags?"

"What was that?" Becky called from the kitchen.

"You picked up the wrong suitcase. I need to go back to the airport."

Becky marched back to Gillian with a theatrical sigh. "Can't we get your suitcase later? You can't just go to lunch like that?"

Gillian looked down at her creased blouse and slacks. She would be comfortable, but her fragile self-esteem would be no match for the highbrow standards and tutting sideways glances of Marcellinas. "I can't go like this."

Becky looked her up and down and huffed. "You're right. Call the airline. We have to go back to the airport."

David leaned his forehead against Julian's office window, the sweat from his brow trickling past the view. The city rushed around below him, unaware and uncaring that his life was evaporating in front of him.

Why is my life always ruined by the mistakes of others?

"I don't care if you've had a major mix-up," David shouted into his phone. "I don't have time to go to the airport. Yes, I suggest you talk to someone. *Fix! This! Problem!*"

David breathed ragged and hard as the airline pushed him back into a holding pattern. He was going to lose his job because Baggage Services couldn't manage the only task they existed to perform.

He was going to lose his job, his purpose—other than Caitlin, his sole source of happiness as he and his wife drifted apart. As Sharon had turned to another man while he worked long days to provide for his family.

David's heavy breath fogged the window, partly obscuring his reflection of Julian, who stretched behind the polished mahogany desk and checked his Rolex. "Ten minutes. What's happening?"

David shook his head and paced the office,

aware of the snarl on his face, held in place by the airline's automated customer service robot. "Thank you for holding. Your call is important to us—"

Right. It's so important you refuse to take it.

With a glance, David could see Julian's eyes following him back and forth across the office. "Can't you wing it?"

David turned on his heel. "Sure, I'm second to none when it comes to thinking on my feet, but my financials paint a clear picture of the exact reason we shouldn't be closed. If I don't have them, all it takes is one question I can't answer, and we'll be dead in the water. The board will be looking for any reason to justify a decision they've probably already made."

Julian cocked an eyebrow. "*We'll* be dead in the water?"

David glared at his boss. The distance he placed between himself and David's fate was becoming more infuriating by the minute. David strode back to the floor-to-ceiling windows before he said something that would make Julian's decision so much easier. He glared at the city instead.

The robot was back in his ear. "Our passengers are our number one priority—"

"Like heck they are!" David thumped his fist on the window.

His breathing accelerated, and panic threatened to burst through his chest. He needed to get back in control, and there was just one way to do it. He closed his eyes and pictured his happiest memory—the day of the ferry cruise just twelve months ago, with Caitlin in pink princess ruffles and Sharon by his side. A rare day off with the wind in his hair and a smile on his lips. On *all* their lips. David's heart slowed its pounding, unbalanced rhythm, and his breathing resumed normal transmission.

He spun around to Julian. Was the desperation he felt flaring in his eyes? "What chance is there we can move my meeting to later this morning? Or this afternoon?"

David detected the hint of a smile from Julian. Yes, his job would be easier with this monumental mistake. "Very little. We've got another eleven branches to fit into the day. I've stacked them around the building like an air traffic controller so they don't run into each other. They're just as anxious as you are about saving their branches."

"But they'll have everything they need. Can't you at least try?" David succeeded—just—in keeping the pleading out of his voice.

Julian stood and shook his head. "It will be nearly impossible, but as a friend I'll see what I can do. It's the least I can do for one of my guys." And with that, he charged out of his office.

My guys? One minute it's "we" and "us" and now it's "my guys"?

A click and a whir chirped down the phone

line. "Thank you for holding, sir." This young man sounded a lot calmer than the other frazzled disembodied voices David had reduced to tears.

"Well?" David's panicked impatience resumed its simmer.

The guy stayed calm, in contrast to his colleagues. "There appears to have been a mix-up with your baggage—"

"So I've heard three times from you people. Tell me something I don't know."

The young man paused. "Well, you need to deal with your baggage, but you're fortunate. We can arrange for it to be at our city depot inside the hour. You'll need to bring with you the bag you've got. Do you have a pen and paper for the address?"

Heat flashed through David as he slammed his hand again against the window. "Fortunate? I have to make a life-or-death presentation in ten minutes, so no, I can't go to some depot somewhere else—"

But the young man was cool and collected. "With respect, sir, it appears the wrong baggage was taken from the carousel, so some part of this situation has to be your responsibility. But let's not argue about fault or blame. It would be good if you could—"

Julian charged into David's conversation, forcing him to mute the call. "Here's the deal: I can slide your presentation back by two hours, but that's it. If you aren't back by then, the leadership will make a decision about your branch without your presentation *or* your financials."

David unmuted the call. "Give me the address."

As the young man dictated the depot's location, David searched Julian's desk for a Post-it note and then scribbled it down.

"Once again, I apologize for this mix-up, sir. I will see you at the—"

David cut the call as he moved to the door. "I've got to find this baggage depot. They said it was in the Docklands development. That's not far, is it?"

Julian shook his head. "It shouldn't take you long to get there."

David stormed out of the office, wheeling the suitcase behind him, muttering under his breath about incompetent airline staff, self-interested corporate shills, his wife, and just for the sake of it, the universe itself. As he marched toward the elevator, Julian's voice echoed down the corridor after him. "You've got two hours, and that's it! You owe me!"

I owe you? It took everything in David's power to keep walking. He mashed the elevator button and stepped back as his phone rang.

Caitlin.

"Daddy!"

He smiled at her high-pitched squeak. "How's my princess?"

"We're going to see the princess show, and I'm going to be a princess, and it's going to be the funnest thing to see all the princesses."

A promise was a promise, even if he'd had to fly across the country to keep the job that would pay for the Disney on Ice tickets.

"That's right, darling. When I get back home after my big trip."

Still no elevator. Anxiety clawed at his neck.

"We're going *today,* Daddy!" David imagined the set of her tiny jaw. She was definitely *his* little princess.

"No, honey, when I come back we'll buy the tickets." David again mashed the elevator button.

She giggled. "And I want to buy a princess tiara, and we're going to have chocolates."

David stifled a laugh before the shadow of panic swooped over his momentary sunny spot on a gray day. "I promise I'll buy the tiara when we go."

The elevator dinged its arrival, and David pushed his way past some exiting suits as he hammered the ground floor button.

"I've got to go, Caitie. I need to find my suitcase for my meeting."

"Bye." *Click.* In an instant she was gone.

David's breathing sped up as the lights slowly flashed his descent. He just had to save his job.

—8—

Gillian could feel Becky fuming as they got into the Audi. Her sister clenched the steering wheel and breathed through her nose like her mother used to when Gillian knew she was in real trouble.

Becky drummed her gloved fingers on the wheel. "So where is this place?"

"In the Docklands development." She recited the address.

Becky unclenched and clenched her grip on the wheel and breathed hard again as she pulled out of the driveway.

Gillian alternated her gaze between the window and the folded hands in her lap. "I'm sorry for this delay, but to be fair, you were the one who grabbed the suitcase off the carousel."

When it came to criticism, Becky was Teflon-coated. "I've never had any problems with my baggage before. Anyway, let's not let your lost baggage bring down our day. We've got to stay positive. It's all planned. We'll still go to lunch at Marcellinas, and we must do the manicures and facials tomorrow afternoon. I've got to look fantastic as the mother of the bride. This will be the third wedding in our tennis club this month."

Gillian looked out the window again, needing

just a moment to breathe. "You didn't answer my question about how Brent is doing. Isn't he involved in any of the wedding arrangements?"

Becky again paused, her brow furrowed as if she were measuring careful words. "No, he's not doing much, but he's working. We'll see him at the rehearsal dinner. Anyway, how's Rick's job? Going well, is it? He's making lots of money?"

Gillian took a deep breath, relieved at getting a second chance to share. "At the moment, he's doing a great job. He's under a lot of pressure, and his bosses are always talking about the possibility of cutting jobs, but he's still there. Coming here for the wedding will be just the break he needs. In fact, we all need it."

"I'm glad you raised it, Gilly, because I wasn't sure how to raise it without offending you, but you're looking a bit tired and you've put on a bit of weight."

Gillian rolled her eyes. "Thanks very much."

"Well, you are, and you have, and I'm worried about you. You haven't looked happy since I picked you up, and I would have thought Jessica's wedding would be a happy occasion for us all."

Gillian choked down any reaction before it escaped and just gave her another problem to fix—another one that wasn't her own doing. "If you'd prefer that I hadn't come early—"

"That's not it at all." Becky peered over her designer sunglasses at her reflection in the mirror.

"Look, let's get your baggage fixed up first, and then we can have a proper talk over some good food at Marcellinas rather than out here in the middle of nowhere."

The landscape outside Gillian's window became sparser with each passing minute. For a new development, it didn't have much to inspire a purchase. Block after block was a dustbowl, dotted with knee-high weeds and occasional construction equipment, abandoned and succumbing to the ravages of time and salty air. Huge cranes stood tall and unmoving, a still life of steel giraffes on a dusty savannah. The only life was the occasional seabird that sailed on the wind and squawked its hunger to no one.

Becky slowed as they approached a lonely bright-white warehouse, standing alone in this urban wasteland. She pulled up outside the building. "Well, this is the address. Are you sure it's the right place?" She grabbed her phone. "Give me the number and I'll check for you."

"No, this is the address they gave me." Gillian was adamant as she hopped out of the car and into the heat.

Becky lowered Gillian's window by an inch. "Well, I'll just wait out here. It shouldn't take too long, I hope." Becky could make her voice sound like it was rolling its eyes.

"No, I hope it doesn't." Gillian took the suitcase from the back seat and crossed the deserted street to the only disruption in the brilliant white facade: a set of glass double doors recessed into the front of the building.

They slid open for her, and she stepped into a reception area that looked like it belonged in a hospital. The room was nothing but white. White pictures in white frames on white walls. White lounge chairs. White vases holding white foliage. A white clock on the wall. And on the white counter, a small white bell, which Gillian rang. It sounded a note like champagne glasses touched for a toast.

As the note dissipated, nothing happened.

"Hello?" She rang the bell again.

A blue sign broke the sheer white in the room: Baggage Services. It hung on the wall, next to a single white door to one side of the white counter.

Gillian could hear movement behind the door, and then its handle turned.

—9—

David dug into his wallet for more cash to ensure he wouldn't be left stranded in this deserted industrial area.

The cab driver extorting money from him clutched the bills in a sweaty hand. "That buys you twenty minutes." He gave an oily smile, and David's suspicions ratcheted up. He just knew this guy would be gone the minute he went into this strange building.

David pulled out his phone and took a photo of the driver and then his ID number, printed on the dashboard for a passenger's peace of mind.

"Just making sure my extra cash will buy me twenty minutes."

The viscous smile oozed from the driver's face.

David stepped out of the cab, and the humidity again enveloped him like a wool blanket. He pulled the crumpled Post-it from his pocket. This was the right address, but there was no way those he'd conversed with earlier worked here. This part of town was abandoned—empty streets and building sites echoed with bird noise, and wind whipped across the industrial plains. As the cab had approached and the buildings had thinned out, David's heart had resumed its pounding rhythm, and the sweat, drawn out of him by baking in the back seat of an un-air-conditioned taxi in summer heat, just as he feared, ran in rivulets down his temples. He winced as the reflection of the sun off this sheer white building burned bright in his eyes. What sort of tin-pot airline had a depot out here in the middle of nowhere?

He charged across the street and scoured both ends of this warehouse, whose white facade stretched wide in both directions. To the left, no doors. To the right, no doors. Both ways, no windows to be seen.

David stomped to one end of the building and whipped around the corner. He stopped in his tracks. Nothing but more unbroken brilliant white and an empty street that led to a fenced dead end and the dockside beyond. And no sign of life.

He stomped back along the building's frontage to the other intersection, sweat now pouring from his brow and down his back. He was walking miles, someone else's suitcase careening behind him in tow, burning time he didn't have. He marched around the corner, confident there would be a door, an entrance, anything. This side of the building, too, stretched down a side street to the docks, but halfway along was a simple garage door, also white, recessed into the building. Next to the roller shutter—a sleek metal curtain of gleaming white, shut tight against the outside world and him—was the only color on the whole building: a dark-blue sign whose white letters announced with pride, Baggage Services!

Finally.

David half sprinted to the roller shutter, now uncaring about the sweat. He looked for a bell, a switch—anything—so he could summon someone to fix this mess. He had less than two hours to get back on track and save his future before a range of faceless men signed his death warrant.

But there was no bell. Except for the sign, there was nothing on the wall at all.

David stood back and scanned up and down the street. This door was his lone option without walking a half mile to the next corner to see what was around the back of this strange, deserted building. What type of operation were they running here?

He rapped hard on the roller shutter, burning his knuckles on white-hot steel. "Hello?"

Nothing.

The roller shutter buckled as David slammed his fist onto it. *"Hello?"* His voice strained with anger on a very short leash. He turned away, punched the airline's number into his phone, and steeled himself as the call rang, ready to give both barrels to another customer service operator pretending to give him personal service while reading from a script.

Then behind him he heard a rattle as the roller

shutter jiggled and then clunked as his call continued to ring. He turned, and the shutter clunked again, and with the chinking of swinging chains and the groan of an aging motor, it started a slow rise. David cut the call.

Brilliant white light came from below the shutter, and David shifted on his feet, his prepared outburst locked and loaded. The shutter rose further, and he stretched his neck, limbering up to deliver the serve someone deserved. He plastered a practiced scowl on his face, the scowl of the righteous wronged.

But the scowl slipped when David saw a familiar face.

—10—

The taxi driver jerked his cab to a stop and threw a meaty, hairy arm across the passenger seat. He spat out the fare. "Twenty-two dollars, kid."

Twenty-two dollars? For a ten-minute ride?

Michael gulped. "Um, are you sure? Coach said it would be twelve dollars."

The driver glanced around the inside of his cab before fixing an oily, dead-eye glare at Michael. "Whoever Coach is, he ain't here, and I'm the one driving. Twenty-two dollars."

Michael stretched his wallet wide, hoping to find spare cash hidden in its leather folds for the first time ever. He sighed as he handed over too many bills. "How will I get back to the university?"

"Not my problem, kid. Maybe this coach you keep talking about can send you the money." The driver jerked his head toward the door.

Fragments of defense rushed around Michael's head—*Give me a break; I'm new in this town*—but they refused to come out.

As the taxi drove away, Michael slipped his near-empty wallet back into his pocket with a heavy sigh. Maybe the people at this baggage place could help him get back to the university. He jumped as R2-D2 chirped in his hand. He looked at his phone with eager anticipation—maybe Coach had found a way for him to get back.

His heart sank. Dad.

Don't forget to mention the videos I've uploaded, Mikey.

Michael shook his head as he swiped away the message. He shielded his eyes as he stood in front of the building, a massive white, almost translucent, warehouse that, in the summer sun, shone like a beacon in an industrial part of the city. It was a construction zone of fences keeping people out of nothing, with empty fields strewn with rubble and discarded, twisted steel. The only sounds were the squawks of seabirds and trash flapping against the chain link. Michael looked to the left, and then the right. This building stretched a full block, but it had no windows or doors. A large blue-and-white sign broke the shining luminosity of this white box with a chunky arrow and a cheesy exclamation point, announcing that Baggage Services was just around the corner.

Wheeling someone else's suitcase behind him, Michael's mind was a blur as his future—immediate and distant—melted before his eyes in the heat. Hardware beckoned once again.

Michael rounded the corner. Again, the building stretched for a full block, and again, he saw no doors or windows. He kept walking, head down, spinning through solutions to his most immediate problem. He came up empty. *How am I going to get back to the university?* Michael stopped and looked over his shoulder. He'd come halfway down the street, and still there were no doors or windows on this side of the building. Had he missed something? Was the arrow pointing the other way? He sighed. He'd come too far to go back to the front of the building and try the other side.

Michael turned to keep walking, and a door now appeared, not ten feet from him. He did a double take. *Where did that door come from? Man, I must have been deep in my thoughts to miss that.* On the door was a small blue-and-white sign: Baggage Services!

Michael pushed open the door and wiped his feet on a fluffy white doormat. He walked into a reception area that was a blast of pristine white. The same blue-and-white sign stood proud on an almost-glowing white reception counter. A man in a navy-blue cap sat behind a desk, head down, buried in paperwork.

Michael stood, waiting for recognition.

There was none.

He rocked back on his heels, thinking movement might force this man to look up, to acknowledge him. But he saw only a slight bobbing of the Baggage Services cap.

Michael broke the silence with an ever-so-slight clearing of his throat, the lowest noise he could make to interrupt but not offend. The cap's peak shot up, and the young man in navy-blue overalls from the airport broke into a broad grin. He stood and tipped his cap as his curly, black hair sprung free across his forehead. "Welcome to Baggage Services. I'm the Baggage Handler. Would you like help with your baggage?"

Michael allowed himself a smile. At least this was a familiar face. Maybe he *could* help.

11

As Michael followed the Baggage Handler down a sheer white corridor studded with white doors, the artist in him shuddered. He was all for white space, but this place was ridiculous. White door after white door, each with just a simple black handle. No signs, no indication of what lay inside, and the long corridor seemed to disappear into a black dot on a shimmering white horizon.

The Baggage Handler jolted to a stop in front of one door, jangled a heavy wad of gold keys from his pocket, and isolated one. He ushered Michael into a waiting room that assaulted his designer's senses after the simplicity of so much white. It was as if a paint shop had exploded, with every color on the spectrum screaming at him for attention in a rainbow cacophony.

A beaten-up, fraying sofa in red-and-brown checks almost apologized as it offered a seat to Michael. On it sat mismatched cushions that threw another three clashes of color into the mix: blue, black, and orange. An old-school TV, all chunky and thick and black, sat atop a stained and dented pine cabinet.

Next to a full-length mirror in a bright-yellow plastic frame stood a sturdy, proud, mustard-yellow fridge whirring and chugging, a throwback to another time and another nod to a different corner of the color palette. On the wall next to it was a clock with an extraordinarily large face and neon-blue hands like Edward Scissorhands's, carving up the day.

Michael shuddered.

The Baggage Handler checked his clipboard. "There appears to have been some identical baggage on your flight. I apologize for any inconvenience. I'm the only one here at the moment, so please make yourself at home. And help yourself." He gestured toward the fridge and headed for the door, whistling a tune that, to Michael, was familiar and yet somehow elusive.

He looked around at the mess of color and the eclectic mix of furnishings, each drawn from its own time and place and thrown together with all the others in hope. "I know I flew with a low-cost airline, but wow!"

The Baggage Handler stopped in his tracks. "I like color. Surely the more of it you have, the better?"

Michael bit his lip. "I'm sorry if I offended you. It's just that I love art and . . ."

The Baggage Handler folded his arms and tapped the clipboard against his chest. "You're an artist? Good for you!"

The hint of a smile crept across Michael's face.

"Do you think you're any good?"

Michael's smile faltered. "My art teacher thinks so."

The Baggage Handler fixed a gaze on him with clouded blue eyes, a look approaching wistfulness. "That wasn't my question. I asked if *you* think you're any good."

The answer to this question lurked just below the surface, but Michael was so used to holding it down. "I . . . I . . . I guess so."

"So why would a young guy like you come to our city? Are you here to see our art gallery?"

"I was hoping to get there somehow later today. I'm visiting Clarendon University to see about a scholarship."

The Baggage Handler's face lit up. "That's amazing! You must be some kind of artist."

The truth won out. "No. It's a track scholarship."

The Baggage Handler's brow furrowed as the light in his face dimmed. "But you're an artist."

The artist within Michael scrambled to break out and bask in the recognition it craved. "Yeah, I know, but my father has set up this trip to talk about a track scholarship—" He shook it off. "Anyway, I won't have a scholarship of any kind unless I can sort this out and get back to the university. How long will this take?"

"Not long." The Baggage Handler hugged the clipboard to his chest. "It depends on you."

Michael cocked his head. What did that mean?

"Here, sign this." The Baggage Handler thrust the clipboard under Michael's nose. He took the pen and, with great care, signed the form.

"Thanks. Back in a minute." The Baggage Handler took the suitcase from Michael and closed the door behind him.

Michael was alone in the strange kaleidoscope of a room. He fell back on the sofa, and it groaned as if it would collapse. He tried for a full minute to get comfortable, but it was impossible. The cushions would have disappointed Goldilocks and all three of her bears: one was too hard, one was too soft, but none of them was just right.

Michael's growling stomach led him to the fridge, which gave a mechanical sigh as it revealed a tray of fresh sandwiches on a shelf. Michael shoved one into his mouth. His stomach was grateful for the reprieve. His taste buds were delighted.

His mouth now stuffed, Michael looked at the inspirational posters on the wall. The first one—a representation of Martin Luther King Jr. as seen through Andy Warhol's eyes—offended his inner designer critic. He read the caption aloud: " 'We must accept finite disappointment, but never lose infinite hope.' " Michael nodded. Great quote; pity about the clichéd artwork.

He moved across to the second poster, a rock climber hanging one-handed from a snow-covered cliff ledge. *Only you know if you're up to the challenge.*

The third poster brought a laugh. An unimpressed bulldog was caught midblink as he looked like he'd swallowed a wasp. *You are you. Embrace it.*

If only.

Michael went back to the fridge to grab another sandwich and left two out of courtesy. He looked at the chunky TV; he hadn't seen one that solid since his grandfather's sitting room, from a time when TVs were furniture. He sank into the sofa and watched the hands of the clock count off minutes he didn't have. Minutes that would see him miss the scholarship. Minutes that would see him working in a hardware store inside a week. A cold fear washed over him as he sat forward, his head in his hands. He checked his phone. No messages from the coach, but then he saw why—no reception.

The specter of his dad's disappointment again hung over him. He dreaded the conversation he would need to have at home, a barrage of "I told you so's" peppered with the usual spiel about disappointment in him.

A conversation whose script he already knew.

One in which he had no lines.

12

Gillian whistled as she stood in the doorway of the waiting room. "Wow, this is slick for a low-cost airline. I wish my family room looked like this."

Along one wall a sleek brown leather couch slung low next to a tall lamp with a dark-green-and-gold-leaf shade. A large mahogany coffee table commanded the room, and on it sat a huge glass bowl overflowing with fresh fruit. Next to it was a crystal decanter of red wine along with two long-stemmed balloon glasses.

A large flat-screen television covered one wall. The voices coming from it were but a murmur, but it had to be a soap opera, with the earnest glances, overreactions, and perfect teeth.

The Baggage Handler followed her, wheeling his baggage cart. On it was the suitcase Gillian had brought back. "Why do you wish your family room looked like this? It's empty."

The leather sofa gave an extravagant sigh as Gillian sank into it. "Empty? This place is perfect. My place is a mess compared to this."

"Mmm." The Baggage Handler nodded as he studied her.

Two huge posters adorned one wall. A tiny, forlorn puppy eyed a bone outside the kennel he moped in. Huge letters gave him an idea of how to fix his problem: *Stop wishing. Start doing.* The poster next to it showed a stunning sunflower in a field of green at dawn, dewdrops dotting its face like morning tears. Gillian read the caption aloud: " 'All flowers are beautiful in their own way, and that's like women too. Miranda Kerr.' "

There was no denying the sunflower was beautiful, standing at attention and dressed in elegant bright yellow, its tearstained face dried by the morning sun.

"That's a lovely thought." Gillian gestured at the poster.

"I agree. We like to carry the right messages in our business." He studied Gillian again. "Do you believe it?"

Gillian didn't know how to answer that question. Next to the sunflower stood a full-length mirror, also framed in rich mahogany. Why would an airline waiting room have a mirror like that? She caught a glimpse of herself on the sofa and whipped her head away, a knee-jerk reflex. She didn't need to be reminded of her flaws. They were tattooed on her soul.

The young man stepped forward. "I've got some paperwork for you, and then we can sort out your baggage." He stopped short. "Are you okay?"

Gillian folded her arms. "I guess so. Why?"

"It's just that you look upset." Gillian shifted

over on the sofa as the Baggage Handler sat down next to her. "I hope you don't mind me saying, but the look on your face just now was one of incredible sadness."

Gillian shook her head. "It's no different to how I look every day."

The Baggage Handler cocked his head and fixed a gaze on her with clouded blue eyes, a look approaching wistfulness. "It's just that I meet lots of people, and I try to help where I can. Can I do anything for you?"

Gillian warmed with his sad concern. This young man had peeked beneath the curtain she put up to keep out the world. "Apart from getting my suitcase, no, but I appreciate you asking."

"No problem. You let me know if you need any help." The Baggage Handler checked his clipboard. "Oh, I see. There appears to have been some identical baggage on your flight. I apologize for any inconvenience. If you'll sign this form, we can help."

Gillian reached for the clipboard. "Great. My sister is out front waiting, and I've been here for five minutes already." She skimmed the form. "What's this?"

"Read it."

" 'I promise to deal with my baggage before I leave this facility.' What an odd form."

"It's just something we need to cover for people to deal with their baggage."

"Deal with?"

The Baggage Handler offered a broad smile to go with his cheeky wink. "Yes, deal with."

"What an odd choice of words. Don't you usually collect your baggage?"

"Yes, people usually collect their baggage, but they'd be better off if they dealt with it. 'Deal with' is exactly what we mean."

There was a beat, a pause in the universe, as that statement settled onto Gillian. It lodged there like an imprint on a sofa. "Well, if you say so. They are just words."

The Baggage Handler shook his head, and his voice took on a passionate edge. "Words have far more power than that." He smiled and pointed to the bottom of the form. "Just there, please."

Gillian signed her name. "Okay, it seems straightforward."

"Thanks very much." The Baggage Handler took back the clipboard and pointed to the suitcase. "Yours looks like this one, but it doesn't have the red embossed leather baggage tags on it."

"No, it doesn't." The memory of Becky grabbing a black suitcase and charging past, leaving her behind on her own trip replayed in her mind. Her shoulders slumped. "My sister grabbed it from the carousel. I wish I'd grabbed my suitcase myself."

The Baggage Handler cocked his head. "Stop wishing. Start doing."

Gillian jolted upright. "Excuse me?"

He gestured to the puppy poster on the wall. "Up there. It sounds like good advice."

Gillian looked sideways at this strange young man as she connected the dots. "You were at the airport, weren't you? In the baggage claim area with a cart?"

The Baggage Handler tipped his cap. "Of course. I was helping people with their baggage."

"You work here as well?"

"I go wherever I'm needed." His cell phone buzzed. "I'll just get your baggage, and then I can help you. Anyway, be back in a minute. Help yourself."

He wheeled the cart out the door, leaving Gillian sitting alone in a perfect waiting room with the perfect fruit bowl on a rich mahogany coffee table and a perfect life playing out on the soap opera on the TV on the wall.

She cast one eye at the puppy poster and sank back into the sofa. This time more than the sofa sighed.

—13—

Each second echoed around David's head as it ticked away. This Baggage Handler guy had asked him to wait, but that moment was forever ago.

Ninety minutes until the new presentation time. Where was this guy? David drummed his fingers on the sofa, the cracked leather catching his skin. He didn't care if this guy was on his own. The airline had messed up his baggage, and they were well on the way to losing him his job as well.

David placed his feet on the black coffee table that sat in the center of the room, stained with coffee mug rings and coated in a thick layer of dust. He stretched back on the jet-black sofa, shiny in parts but cracking along the seams, letting go of its stuffing as if it couldn't contain it anymore.

Down one side of the room, a glossy white counter ran along the wall. On it sat a bronze alarm clock from another time, its hands standing proud but tired against a burnished and worn face. At the end of the counter, a full-length mirror surrounded by a black steel frame lurched to one side, knocked around once too often. The ceiling and walls of the waiting room pulsed with glossy white, but the furniture was falling apart.

The room must be the smoker's lounge; the bitter residue of smoke clung to every surface.

David shook his head at the lack of professionalism. What sort of operation filled one of its main rooms—the ones on show to the world—with furniture that needed urgent attention?

They had stayed true to one corporate expectation. On the far wall, an obligatory inspirational poster was the only color in this monochrome room. But unlike the usual suspects of topics that preached about discipline or persistence, this poster featured one word: *forgiveness*. A tiny bluebird, its escape from an ugly black cage captured midflight, sat above a solemn pronouncement: *To forgive is to set a prisoner free and realize the prisoner was you.* David shook his head again. Best to leave those inspirational quotes to those corporate team-building weekends.

David turned to his phone for distraction as the seconds continued to leak away. He flung Angry Birds around, and his knees bounced along with his impatience. He exhaled his frustration.

Another three minutes smoldered into ash.

When you need to get a job done properly, you have to do it yourself.

He stood up with a rush, strode to the door, threw it open, and peered down the corridor, searching for signs of the kid who had disappeared. He saw nothing but a long white corridor, punctuated by white door after white door, disappearing into a black dot on the horizon, not a soul to be seen.

What was this place? Who in the twenty-first century didn't slap their branding and corporate colors all over their offices?

David looked left and then right, expecting movement. Expecting something. Nothing came.

"Hello?" A single voice came back to him from down the corridor.

His own.

David huffed as he retreated to the sofa and again pulled out his phone. He would need an extension on his presentation time the way things were going. This incompetent airline had already chewed a quarter of the two hours of grace he had. He punched in Julian's direct line but was greeted with a businessman's greatest fear: no phone service. The veins on his temple throbbed hard.

The door handle creaked, and David cricked his neck, a warm-up to deliver some customer feedback to this Baggage Handler. Whistling, the young man stepped back into the room, and David unloaded.

"What on earth is going on here? I had two hours to get back to the head office, and you left me in here for thirty minutes in this joke of a waiting room."

Anger pulsated from David as he unleashed.

But nothing he said landed. The young man in the navy overalls and cap simply stood in silence, hands clasped as if David's tirade was water off a duck's back. David stopped to take a breath.

The Baggage Handler tipped his cap with one hand and clutched his clipboard with the other. "Are you done?"

David was prepared for apologetic, groveling defense, and he was prepared for blame-shifting attack. What he wasn't prepared for was an almost uninterested dismissal of his anger. His mouth flapped open and shut like a goldfish on a sidewalk.

The Baggage Handler checked his clipboard. "There appears to have been some identical baggage on your flight. I apologize for any inconvenience."

"Inconvenience?" David threw his hands up in the air in fuming frustration. "Your monumental mess-up could cost me my career."

The Baggage Handler cocked his head. "Actually, if you don't deal with this, it's going to cost you far more than that."

What on earth did that mean? David clutched his forehead. "What? I need to get out of here. My suitcase wasn't exactly the same as others; I had red luggage tags from my alumni—"

"But that was the problem. Several identical bags had red tags. It always staggers me how so much baggage looks the same, but people do

86

nothing about it." He looked at the suitcase next to David and chuckled to himself. "Why not just get a red suitcase?"

David stepped forward, his pointed finger zeroed in on the Baggage Handler's chest. "Look, buddy. I need you to fix this problem so I can get back to work. I've got a very important meeting. Missing it is going to cost me my job and the jobs of the fifteen people who work under me in our branch. I can't afford to lose any more time."

The Baggage Handler fixed a gaze on David with clouded blue eyes, a look approaching wistfulness. "I know. Your baggage is slowing you down."

David closed his eyes and exhaled hard through clenched teeth at this strange man with the sad eyes. "What are you talking about?" The veins in his temple throbbed again. His stomach gripped him. Again.

The Baggage Handler nodded at the space behind him. "You're dragging it around everywhere with you, and it's stopping you from doing so many things."

David reeled. This strange young man looked like a kid but spoke like a wizened old man. Berating him wasn't working. He needed another plan of attack. His mind fumbled for the right words to use just to get out of this place. He breathed his frustration back deep within him and pressed it down as far as it would go. "All I want to do is deal with my baggage—"

"Great! I want you to deal with it too." The Baggage Handler thrust the clipboard under David's nose. "I need you to sign this, and then I can grab your baggage for you."

David snatched the pen on offer and scrawled a hasty signature at the bottom of the page. "Do I need to jump through any other hoops?"

"I'll just get your baggage." He waved his hand toward the white counter. "Help yourself." He placed the suitcase onto his baggage cart and disappeared again into the corridor, whistling to himself.

David looked at the empty counter. Help yourself? What on earth was this guy talking about? He shot another glance at the tiny bluebird who had escaped his cage. Lucky so-and-so.

—14—

The sharp tang of dust assaulted Michael as he fumbled behind the chunky TV for the remote control. It wasn't there either. It was missing, another disappointment in this strange room.

He wanted—no, needed—a distraction as the seconds ticked away.

He turned on the TV by hand, and the black of the screen flickered into a shimmering gray. Then, through a checkerboard of static, a man appeared, slumped in a leather chair as if the world had beaten him into submission. His sagging suit clung to him almost in apology, and his eyes flitted around the TV studio beneath lowered lids, apparently seeing everyone but also no one.

Sitting across from him was a familiar face: Dr. Gabe, trusted confidant dispensing homespun wisdom to millions, a ratings bonanza dispensing cash for TV executives. The man was a knowing toothy smile and chiseled haircut in a suit jacket and T-shirt, piercing eyes hidden behind half-shell glasses that could pinpoint emotional pain from twenty paces.

Dr. Gabe eased back in his leather chair, his eyeglasses perched on the tip of his nose like an old-school principal's would. He stroked his chin as he sized up the wreck of a man sitting opposite him.

Michael munched away on his last sandwich, the saltiness of the ham and the tang of tomato biting into his tongue. Say what you like about their decorator, but their caterer was great!

Dr. Gabe tapped his top lip with a forefinger, a thought-provoking posture that flagged to his millions of viewers that life's answers were imminent. "What you're telling me, then, is that you're terrified of doing anything with your life because you're sure you will fail."

The man's head snapped up, his stare on high beam like a deer in headlights. "That's not what I said."

Dr. Gabe slipped off his glasses and pointed them at his patient. "But that's what your body language is screaming out to me."

Michael, suddenly self-conscious, sat taller on the sofa to hide his slouch.

"And it's disagreed with everything you've said so far. But may I give you some advice?" A rhetorical question. The advice was coming anyway.

The man offered a meek nod above the arms he'd crossed as a wall of defense.

"You *will* fail."

The man's arms relaxed under the spotlight of truth. People in the audience gasped as they edged forward on their seats.

Dr. Gabe wasn't finished with him. "It's a self-fulfilling prophecy you're doomed to repeat." Heads nodded across the studio audience and applause rippled across the seats in appreciation at this golden nugget of insight.

Dr. Gabe cocked his head and changed tack. "What do you do for a living?"

The man mumbled his response into his chest. "I work in sales."

Michael skulked to the fridge for another sandwich, his eyes glued to the TV.

Dr. Gabe again tapped his top lip with a forefinger. "No, that's what you do for a job. I asked you what you do for a living."

The man threw a confused look at the studio audience, then the camera, where it crashed into the confused look Michael threw at the screen.

"What do you mean?"

"What you do every day . . . Does it fulfill you?"

The man gave a pathetic shrug. "Not in the slightest. I despise it."

Dr. Gabe leaned into the man with a conspiratorial whisper. "Then why do you do it?"

Michael made this a three-way discussion. "Yeah, why?"

Dr. Gabe pointed his glasses at his patient in accusation. "You're miserable, and yet you keep doing what makes you miserable. Does that make any sense to you?"

With a slow shake of the man's head, tears sprang free.

"What do you want to do with your life?"

"I want to be an artist." Michael answered by reflex and then pulled himself up short. *What am I doing? I'm talking to a TV show.*

Dr. Gabe continued his cross-examination. "How old are you?"

The man wiped away the tears and stared hard at his shoes. "Thirty-seven."

Michael's chewing slowed as his future materialized in front of him. *This could be me in twenty years' time.* The thought lodged under his skin like a splinter and prodded him to reach for his comfort zone—his happy place, which was always stocked with graphite pencils and sketch pads. His memory flicked through his portfolio and his drawings, and they did their usual trick as he settled. He flicked through portraits of himself, his mother, his art teacher, wildlife from his backyard, his mother's hands, his girlfriend, Jack Nicholson, his mother . . .

Dr. Gabe zeroed in on the man opposite him. "You tell me you've turned down opportunities to write music, which is your passion, not because you're bad at it, but because you've been told your whole life that writing music isn't a smart career choice."

The eyes of the man on the TV couch welled with more tears. Michael fought to hold back a rising tide of emotion. He glanced around again for the remote—to change the channel, to turn it off. To stop the discomfort.

Dr. Gabe threw his hands wide. "I've got some good news for you. I'm here to tell you that's not the case. Let me ask you something: what would you say to your seventeen-year-old self?"

The man fought back tears. "I'd say believe in yourself and that your dad's not going to make decisions for you."

A chunk of tomato fell from Michael's open mouth and landed in his lap. The studio audience whooped its genuine, spontaneous response to the applause sign.

"Let me tell you something." Dr. Gabe replaced his glasses and leaned forward, hand on hip, chin in hand—a sure sign the advice was about to reach its climax of wisdom before a cut to commercial.

"Yes?" Again Michael responded by reflex and leaned forward.

"People all over our country are missing out on life, not because they can't achieve their dream, but because they're forced to live someone else's."

The camera swept across the studio, capturing the occasional tear and several knowing nods. Michael nodded along with them.

Dr. Gabe stared down the barrel of the camera, right at Michael. "Including you."

Michael's jaw froze as he was caught in the doctor's steely-eyed gaze.

"The message today is that if you're self-sabotaging your future, it's not because you want to, but because that future may not be yours."

The audience again whooped its appreciation as Dr. Gabe broke eye contact with Michael and hugged his patient in an awkward embrace. He discarded the man and faced the faithful. "We'll be back after the break to talk to Jenny, who believes she has failed her children because just three of them are doctors. Join us for 'Why you should stop with mother guilt.'"

Michael lifted the piece of tomato from his leg, Dr. Gabe's words ringing in his ears. His drawings were good. Maybe his art teachers *were* right. He *did* have talent. Michael allowed the slightest sense of achievement and a feeling of pride.

Two football players on the TV screen scowled at Michael and then turned to face each other. They scowled again and were obliterated by an exploding stamp across their faces that announced the Tigers would destroy the Rams this week at the Dome. The advertisement for the upcoming football game crushed sprouting pride in his artistic ability as his dad trampled back into his thoughts.

He quickly returned to his refuge and flicked through his mental design portfolio again. But now his drawings looked bland, the color washed from the pages. The pencil strokes more hesitant and less sharp. The poses he'd sketched less intriguing and more derivative than they'd looked five minutes ago.

He was looking at them through different eyes.

Critical eyes.

Eyes that didn't understand the value of art, the sweep of the pencil, the detail he'd spent hours crafting or the emotion he'd been mining.

Eyes that belonged to his father.

Maybe Dad was right.

—15—

David paced the waiting room like an innocent death row inmate sweating on a last-minute reprieve. Where in the heck was this guy? Another fifteen minutes had been sucked out of his day, and the countdown to the board presentation sped up.

When you need to get a job done properly, you have to do it yourself.

He threw open the door and stepped into the gleaming white corridor that seemed to stretch into infinity in both directions.

"Hello?" Still, the only voice in the corridor was his.

He ground his teeth. *"Hello?"* David screamed at the top of his lungs. Nothing.

This is ridiculous.

David stepped across the corridor and tried a black handle, which refused to budge. Locked. He shook his head and moved down to the next white door. Its handle refused to budge as well.

As he made his way down the corridor, handle after handle resisted him. An uneven pounding built in his chest, and his frustration grew with each failure. He crossed the corridor and tried one more handle. Locked. He growled in frustration as he ripped his hand from it, sweat greasing his palms. He shut his eyes and breathed deep in a desperate attempt to regain control as the day swirled faster and faster around the drain.

David looked back down the corridor from where he'd come. His mind backflipped at a corridor that disappeared into the distance, each door like the one before it and the one after. His pulse thumped in his ears as a numbing realization swept through him. *I have to get back, but through which door?*

His heart still pounded, and his breathing threatened to run away from him like a wild horse on a prairie. His stomach growled its frustration. David reached into his pocket for an antacid and popped his last one into his mouth.

How many doors had he tried? Four? Six? Twenty? Looking down an infinite corridor of doors, it might as well have been a hundred.

David squeezed his eyes shut to push down a rising sense of panic—an unwelcome emotion. The anxiety pushed him into light-headedness. *Calm down. Calm down.* His rational side waded through the rising tide of his confusion. *All you need to do is head back in the direction you came and try doors until you find one that opens.* Then, as he looked down the corridor that disappeared into the horizon, his rational side tried to make sense of it, threw up its hands, and waded back out of the conversation.

Opening his eyes, David managed to keep an

unstable lid on his emotions. He strode back down the corridor and counted out five doors. This was the one. He turned the handle with confidence and stepped forward, expecting to walk into his waiting room. Instead he walked face-first into another door that refused to budge.

His breath caught. *Calm down. Calm down.*

He tried the door next to it and met a similar result. Then a third and a fourth.

The panic threatened to engulf him, and he screamed.

"Hello? Where are you people?"

People . . . People . . .

Silence followed the echo. The corridor spun as the light-headedness threatened to shut him down.

"What on earth is going on here?"

On here . . . On here . . .

David's anxiety was now joined by a rising sense of indigestion as his stomach attempted to climb out his mouth for its own look at what was going on. He slammed his fists into the nearest white door and shot glances both ways at this impossible corridor. He sank to his knees and screamed, a guttural shriek from the depths of himself. It echoed to both ends of the corridor and reverberated back through him, the vibrations shaking him to his very core.

I have to get back.

David closed his eyes and tried to picture his

family on the ferry as the vibrations dissipated and soaked into the walls. His breathing slowed, and the thumping in his temples slowed as well, as Caitlin's laugh chased away the echoing silence of the corridor.

David regained control and stood as he took a deep breath. He placed his hand on the handle. The door popped open with a gentle click, and David clamored back into the waiting room he had come to think of as his, slamming the door behind him. He sat down on the edge of the sofa, his left hand quivering with a growing tic. Habit forced him to his phone. How had he spent ten minutes out there? He tried to breathe back his self-control, but it wasn't enough. Unable to stay seated, he paced, thinking movement would help him combat the anxiety strangling him.

But the room had changed. The slick white counter that spanned one wall of the waiting room was now stocked with a steaming silver coffee machine, a fruit bowl, and a newspaper. A handwritten sign stood next to it: Help Yourself.

But still no sign of his suitcase. Why would they bring coffee but not his suitcase? David closed his eyes, on the verge of angry tears.

A heady coffee cloud drifted over and enticed him to medicate his tension away. He bypassed the fruit and headed straight for the machine, punched in a triple espresso, and as the machine sputtered and whirred its wizardry, his eyes drifted to the folded newspaper. DIVORCE RATE SPIRALS UPWARD, the front page screamed at him.

I wonder why.

The unfamiliar panic of the corridor was replaced by a more familiar bedrock—anger. He flipped the newspaper, and the headline below the fold screamed at him: SCIENTISTS DISCOVER HOLDING A GRUDGE COULD KILL YOU.

He took the tiny cup from the machine and perched again on the sofa. Where was this guy? David's anger was diluted by an unfamiliar sense of helplessness. He glanced at the door, and the idea of going back out flitted past him. No chance.

The siren call of the newspaper headlines wouldn't be denied. He grabbed the newspaper, and the front page was blunt. Divorce rates in the country were at epidemic levels, and psychologists put it down to the stress of finances, work, and modern society. David huffed. *And I wonder how many divorces are because of wives who cheated on their husbands?* A church leader lamented the growing number of broken families and pleaded with couples to stay together for the sake of their children.

Another unwelcome feeling joined the anxiety in the broiling whitewater of David's emotions: the first twinge of guilt over finding Caitlin with her treasured Disney figurines under her bed after another screaming match he'd had with Sharon. He'd tried to shield his daughter from everything, but he didn't want to think about how much she'd suffered since he discovered the photo on Sharon's phone six months ago.

A sinking feeling settled in his stomach, a deep ache he was finding harder to push away. He flipped over to the second article. A university study had discovered people holding on to grudges suffered physical damage. Anger and unforgiveness affected everything from the flow of chemicals around the body to brain wave interruption, leading even to increased risk of disease or the inability to think and function clearly.

In a photo a university professor stood proudly in front of his sandstone building: "We've found that people who don't forgive end up not only punishing themselves mentally and emotionally but also physically."

Nowadays you can get research to say anything you need it to.

But the next line read like a doctor's diagnosis. "People who stay angry suffer through heart palpitations, headaches, and digestive issues."

David threw the newspaper to the floor. This was just the latest psychobabble designed to keep university types relevant in the twenty-first century. But his stomach wasn't on the same page. It twinged, and by instinct, he reached for his antacids. But the ever-present aluminum square holding the pills was empty.

His eye caught that last paragraph again and interrupted his self-assured dismissal. Surely the stomach issues were a sign of stress? He'd been fighting to keep his job for months, so that had to be it. He scanned his memory further and came up with something slightly more than nothing. A nagging thought perched itself at the back of his mind, a thought he could neither read nor dismiss. It caught on his conscience like a saddle burr. It was tiny and microscopic, but its presence profound. He tumbled it over, analyzing it for an element of truth. Was something there?

The door to the waiting room opened.

16

The leather sofa squeaked under Gillian as she tried, unsuccessfully, to reach for patience. Twenty minutes had gone by. She shuddered to think of the havoc it was playing with Becky's meticulous schedule and the effect that would catch her in its ripples.

Her stomach growled; it had been a few hours since her meager breakfast on the flight. The fruit on the coffee table shone a beacon to her hunger. The apples gleamed with a waxy shine, and the bananas were a stunning bright yellow. She'd never seen fruit quite this bright and luscious-looking before. *Well, the Baggage Handler did tell me to help myself.*

As she reached for the fruit, the grapes gave away the truth. They, too, had a waxy shine, but down the side of one of them was a line, a seam.

Gillian picked up the grape and examined it, feeling the slickness of plastic under her fingers. She squeezed air out of it with a rush and picked up a second grape. Plastic. She dropped an apple on the coffee table, producing an empty, dull thud. With a soundless bounce it rolled onto the carpet and came to rest, a telltale hole in the bottom revealing its molded creation.

Gillian flicked the decanter with a fingernail

and heard the dull clunk of plastic. She removed the stopper, and instead of heady red wine vapor, the familiar tang of grape juice enveloped her. She clinked one balloon glass against the other. Another dull clunk. Plastic. Everything on this table was fake.

She poured the grape juice into the plastic "glass." She laughed to herself. This is a low-cost airline, all right.

Gillian settled back into the sofa, the leather creaking under her. Her upward glance caught her reflection in the mirror. She scooched down in a hurry, out of her own eyeline, and looked instead at the TV on the wall. She lifted a remote and punched up the volume on the soap opera.

"But, Ranch, I can't love you when I'm in love with your twin brother." The brunette with the heaving bosom walked past her costar toward the camera and stared off into the middle distance over Gillian's shoulder.

Ranch moved in behind the brunette and placed his hands on her bare shoulders. An emotive piano tinkled away. "Kourtnay, my love, my soul mate. I'm not Ranch, nor am I his twin brother, French." A string concerto joined the piano as the music swelled and drew Gillian into the soap opera's manufactured pain. "I am their long-lost triplet, Caesar." The music climbed to a crescendo; a final, moody piano chord hung out to dry as the screen faded to black.

Gillian jumped as her senses were assaulted by pulsing graphics and thumping dance music. "In this week's edition of *Perfect Woman* magazine, has Taylor Swift finally had a bad hair day? We have the photos!" The voice-over grated on Gillian's nerves as an unflattering portrait of pop royalty getting off a plane in a windstorm was smeared across the screen.

Gillian's hand patted down her own hair out of reflex. *That's pretty unfair.*

"Ten ways for you to look fantastic 24/7!" A woman rolled over in bed to reveal a perfect, lipsticked smile and a cheesy thumbs-up. "Our celebrity makeover judges give you the tips to look fabulous at any time of the day or night!"

Gillian shook her head. No one with kids looked like that. Did they?

"And we'll fulfill every woman's dream by revealing the makeup secrets that will catch the eye of every man in town!"

As she sipped her juice, Gillian racked her brain for *one* woman she knew for whom that was a dream. She came up empty.

"All in this week's edition of *Perfect Woman* magazine! Out now!"

On the screen, popcorn spilled across a carefully groomed rug.

Now that's more like the real world.

Three boys wearing crisp jeans, white T-shirts, and impossibly perfect tousled mops of blond hair bounced on the sofa in a family room. Their mother swept in, her hair perfect, her makeup immaculate. "Boys!" An ever-so-slightly disapproving look drifted across her face as she pulled a steaming muffin tray from behind her back. "Who's the best mom on the street?"

"You are!" the boys shrieked as they raced over to her, grabbed a muffin the size of a small Volkswagen, gave her an energetic hug, and sped off to the kitchen table.

The mother sighed in triumph—another job well done—as a deep male voice floated across the scene of domestic bliss. "Sweet Dreams muffins. Do you want to be the best mom on the street?"

Mom turned to the camera and smiled widely.

The voice-over continued. "Well, do you, Gillian?"

Mom winked.

Gillian dropped the grape juice on the carpet. She stared at the television. *What?*

The brunette with the heaving bosom was back and spun on her heel. "Caesar? Ranch said the rest of his family died in the plane crash that gave him the inheritance to build that school for bikini models."

A faint whistle came from behind the door, a tune familiar and yet somehow elusive. The door opened, and the Baggage Handler strolled through, pushing a baggage cart loaded with a suitcase. Gillian recognized her travel agent's logo on the red baggage tags and sighed in relief. The Baggage Handler spun the baggage cart, took off the suitcase, and placed it in front of her.

"Thank you so much for sorting out my baggage." Gillian moved to pick up the suitcase.

"My pleasure, ma'am." The Baggage Handler tipped his cap.

Gillian grabbed the handle and smiled at the Baggage Handler as he stepped aside, but the suitcase wouldn't move. It was stuck to the floor, impossible to lift.

She let go of the suitcase and stood back, confused. "Are you sure this is my baggage?"

"Of course. Check the tags."

Gillian bent down and read her name and address, written in her hand on the travel agent's tags.

"And the barcode on the side of the suitcase."

Gillian checked this as well. Her name again. This was definitely her suitcase.

She stood back and studied it. She attempted again to lift it, but still it wouldn't move. It weighed a ton; she could never pick it up, let alone carry it. She stood back and folded her arms. "What have you done to my suitcase? Someone has put something in it."

The Baggage Handler fixed a gaze on Gillian

with clouded blue eyes, a look approaching wistfulness.

"You're right there. Why don't you unlock it and have a look inside?"

17

Gillian walked a slow circle around her suitcase. She flicked the baggage tags and stepped back. The Baggage Handler gestured at the suitcase with his hand.

"I'm not opening it!" she told him.

The Baggage Handler checked his clipboard. "Well, I can't open it. You're the only one who can."

Gillian shook her head. She couldn't stand here and argue with Becky waiting, so she tried to lay down her baggage. There was a weight in it, a heaviness that fixed it to the floor. She gave it a shove, and it teetered on its edge and settled back into position. She pushed hard, and it toppled and fell with a heavy thud, rippling a shudder through Gillian's feet. The Baggage Handler looked at the suitcase, his face a picture of unbridled joy.

She snapped open her lock and clicked the zipper—slowly—as she ran through the options. Someone had put something heavy in her baggage. How could they do that? Obviously, it wasn't anything illegal; otherwise she would have been stopped at the airport. It wouldn't be dangerous, because the Baggage Handler was still standing there. There was no way she had packed anything remotely that heavy in her baggage, and even if she had, she wouldn't have been allowed to check it.

Who put something in there? Rick? Was it a surprise to help her survive Hurricane Becky?

She carefully lifted one corner of the suitcase lid and peered into the darkness. She saw a flash of familiar duck-egg blue; her cocktail dress—the one Rick had insisted she wear to the wedding reception—was still there. That was a relief. As she carefully peeled away the lid of her suitcase, she saw her makeup case nestled under her favorite navy scarf. She flung the suitcase open. It was the same as when she packed it.

Except for one thing.

Sitting on top of her clothes was an item foreign to her: a beautifully crafted, ornate, silver hand mirror.

This is what was making my suitcase so heavy?

Gillian pointed at the mirror. "Um, whose is that?"

The Baggage Handler leaned in and had a look. "You checked that this baggage is yours, right?"

"Yes, I did."

"And you packed it yourself?"

"Who are you? You sound like airport security."

"Then it must be yours."

Gillian gestured to this intruder in her suitcase. "But I've never seen that before. I didn't bring it with me on my trip."

110

The Baggage Handler placed his clipboard on the counter, rocked back on his heels, and shoved his hands into his pockets. "You take it everywhere with you, Gillian. I suggest you have a closer look."

Gillian reached in and nudged the mirror. Nothing happened, although what would it do? Rise up and float in the air? Her fingertips brushed the raised silver relief of a beautiful woman, who could have been a Greek goddess, with flowing hair and a crown of flowers. She was surrounded by a motif of swirling ribbons and bouquets. The ribbons framed the back of the mirror and twisted their way down the handle, where they met, crossed over, and wrapped around the tiniest engraving. Two words in Victorian script had been scratched into the facade with a practiced hand.

Gillian knelt over the suitcase and adjusted her glasses. The two words came into focus. The script was a name.

Her name.

She looked up at the Baggage Handler, her mouth open. "But I've never seen this before. Did Rick buy this for me?"

The Baggage Handler fixed a gaze on Gillian with clouded blue eyes, a look approaching wistfulness. "No. He tries to stop you using it, but you use it every day."

"What do you mean I use it every day? I've

never seen this before in my life." She curled her fingers around the mirror and lifted it gently from her suitcase. The mirror was light as a feather. This wouldn't keep her from picking up her suitcase.

Gillian put the mirror on the sofa and leaned back over the suitcase, ready to rummage for the source of the extra weight in her baggage.

But the Baggage Handler stopped her with a hand. "Look at the mirror, Gillian. Flip it over."

Gillian turned the mirror over and regretted it in an instant. She looked beyond exhausted. Heavy black bags hung under her eyes, her hair was flying in all directions, and her blouse was badly creased. She threw the mirror back into the suitcase, but it didn't land on her blue cocktail dress. It bounced and settled on a handful of photos she hadn't seen when she found the mirror.

"I didn't put these in here either." Her hand froze as she started to pick up the first photo. A house. Her house. Through five-feet-high weeds dotting the front yard, Gillian could see her home was falling apart, its paint peeling away and the shutters hanging on for dear life. Junk mail was scattered across the porch. Tiny patches of green lawn struggled to rise above a sea of brown.

Gillian looked up at the Baggage Handler, unasked questions in her eyes. He nodded toward the suitcase.

She picked up another photo. Her family room was strewn with toys, discarded sports uniforms, and socks. Pillows were scattered across stained carpet; fingerprints were smeared along the black screen of the family's television. Muddy footprints ran through the room. She picked up the next photo. Her women's group from church was sitting around their regular table at CJ's Café, but they all scowled, boredom written large. *At which meeting was everyone so upset to be there? Did I miss that morning?* But there she was, in the corner of the photo. Sitting glumly at a table. On her own.

She looked back at the Baggage Handler, trying to form words. "What is . . ."

The Baggage Handler gestured to the open suitcase with his head. "There's one more."

Gillian picked up the last photo. It was a photo of her family, in a traditional portrait shot. And this, like the other photographs, was one the photographer should have been embarrassed to keep. A cross-eyed Tyson poked out his tongue; James punched Alex in the stomach, while his twin's hands clasped around his neck. Gillian stood behind her sons, scolding them with a pointed finger and a frown. And Rick, disappointment plastered on his face, had turned away, looking like he wanted to walk out of the photo.

Gillian waved a trembling photo at the Baggage Handler, tears pricking the corners of her eyes. Her voice reduced to a quavering whisper. "What is this?"

The Baggage Handler sighed, compassion flaring in his eyes. "This is your life, Gillian."

"When were these taken?"

"Yesterday. The day before. Every day. These are the images you carry around with you in your baggage every single day."

"Who would take photos like this?"

"You've asked an excellent question."

Gillian pointed to the photos scattered in the suitcase as sobs rose in her throat. "Why is my house so run down? Why does my husband look like he wants to walk away from his family? Why is everyone in my women's group so miserable?" The tears caught on her glasses, and she pushed the frames up onto her forehead to rub her eyes.

"They're not." The Baggage Handler knelt beside her. "That's just how you see them. Look again."

Gillian glanced at the photo in her hand. Everyone was now smiling, the boys' headlocks now loving arms around shoulders, and Rick had his arm around his wife. He was a proud father standing guard over his family.

Gillian's heart skipped a beat. She staggered back to the sofa in shock and collapsed onto it.

Her glasses dropped back onto her nose. She looked down at the photo again. Her family had gone back to frowning and fighting, and Rick was again looking for the door.

18

"Dah dah dah, dah dah dahhh."

David couldn't place the tune that wafted in through the open door. It was both familiar and yet elusive. He was *sure* he'd heard it before. Hundreds of times before.

"Dah dah dah, dah dah dahhh." Whistling, the Baggage Handler strolled into the waiting room.

David scanned the black suitcase on the cart the Baggage Handler trailed behind him, searching for confirmation. This time it was the right flash of red: his alumni baggage tags, the mighty Rams.

"Finally." David rose from the sofa. This mix-up had cost him an hour of his precious two-hour extension. "You will be hearing from my lawyer."

The Baggage Handler shrugged as he spun the cart and placed the baggage in front of David. He tipped his Baggage Services cap and stood, maddeningly silent.

David exhaled his frustration. "Would you like to help me get out of this place?"

"I'd love to." The Baggage Handler stood back with a sweep of his arm toward the door. "After you."

David strode forward and grabbed the handle

of his suitcase—and almost pulled his arm out of its socket as the baggage remained stuck to the floor. He rubbed his throbbing shoulder and then looked at his suitcase, at the Baggage Handler, and at the suitcase again. He wrapped his fingers around the handle and again tried to lift it, but it wasn't moving. It was glued to the ground. His pulse thumped in his ears, and his stomach grumbled under the stress of yet another delay.

"What is going on here? What have you done to my suitcase?"

The Baggage Handler checked his clipboard. "Nothing. You can check the baggage tags if you like."

"I know it's mine! Those are my baggage tags! What have you people done? Why can't I lift it?"

The Baggage Handler shrugged. "You saw me lift it with no problem. And it's locked."

David tried again to lift his suitcase, but it still wasn't moving. He closed his eyes and breathed hard. Then the reason for this entire shambles of a trip dawned on him. It was the only rational explanation. No car at the airport. A sweaty, incense-infused cab ride. Someone else's bag. Now this.

The smallest laugh escaped his lips. He knew what was going on.

"Okay, enough already! If this is some kind of prank for a TV show . . ." He shot glances into every corner of the room, looking for hidden cameras in the ceiling, in the fruit bowl, anywhere. "You've got hidden cameras somewhere. Congratulations, you got me." He bowed to the fruit bowl, where he was sure the hidden camera was. "Whoever has put up this prank, you can come out now. Julian? I presume it's you."

It was the only explanation that made sense.

But the Baggage Handler hadn't moved. "What are you talking about, David?"

"Well, it's obvious this is a prank. That explains everything. I fly into the city for a meeting, but somehow my suitcase is mixed up. There isn't a limousine waiting for me. Head office treats me like some kind of leper. I go to a strange depot in the middle of nowhere instead of to the airport, and then I'm left here in a waiting room for an hour. I head out to the corridor to find someone, and it's like I'm stuck in the Matrix or something. And then when you bring my suitcase back, it's impossible to pick up."

David leaned across to the Baggage Handler in a whisper. "You were pretty impressive, by the way. Mysterious, talking like a karate master and appearing at both the airport and the depot. Well done!"

The Baggage Handler looked at David with piercing blue eyes that bored into his soul. "This isn't a prank."

David folded his arms. "Well, what's going on, then?"

"Why do you think you can't pick up your baggage?"

David threw his hands into the air. "And stop calling it baggage. It's a suitcase! Anyway, why can't I lift it? It wasn't heavy when I checked it at the airport."

"I think you'll find your baggage has always been heavy. That's why it weighs you down."

David again exhaled heavily. "Will you stop talking as if you're Confucius or a Facebook meme or whatever? You've obviously put something in there. What's going on here?"

The Baggage Handler spoke in a near-whisper, a counterpoint to David's simmering anger. "Why are you asking me? You're a man of action. Why don't you look for yourself?"

David stood back and folded his arms again. "No. If I open it, it will explode in my face or something. I don't trust you. You open it."

But the Baggage Handler sat down on the sofa and crossed his legs. "I can't. I'm also not the one in a hurry, David. It's your baggage."

"Okay, fine, whatever. Anything to get out of this place." David toed the suitcase, and it sat solid on the floor. Immovable. He shoved it again, and it gave a gentle rock before settling back into position. With one almighty push, it rocked past the point of no return and slammed onto the floor.

David bent over and thumbed in the lock's

combination. As he unzipped the bag, his gaze never left the Baggage Handler. "Well, let's see what we've got in here, shall we?" He eased open the lid with a careful eye and breathed again. His much-needed financial reports sat on top of his few overnight clothes. But his eye was caught by something on top of the reports. Something unexpected. Two ferry tickets, a few restaurant receipts, and a man's polo shirt, which wasn't his. He picked it up. "This isn't—"

"Just look at it."

On the collar was a mark: bright-pink lipstick. David looked back at the Baggage Handler, who gestured toward David's suitcase with his head. "Have a closer look."

One more extra thing was there. A printed photograph—a selfie of two people kissing while sitting in the sun on the back of a ferry, the wind in their hair, sea spray on their faces.

Two people enjoying the sun and the scenery. Two people enjoying each other.

His wife was one of them, but he wasn't the other.

It was Jerry, his former best friend.

The exact photo he'd found on Sharon's phone six months ago.

—19—

A familiar tune floated in from the corridor, drawing Michael into an instinctive matching whistle. Where had he heard that before?

The door flung open, and the Baggage Handler wheeled in a cart. "I've got your baggage." He spun it in front of Michael. "Apologies once again." He placed the suitcase on the floor with a flourish and stepped back, rubbing his hands together with glee.

"Thanks." Michael stepped forward in a rush and grabbed the handle of his suitcase. But the suitcase stayed steadfastly where it was. His body continued moving while his hand stayed connected to the suitcase, and his legs flew into the air. With a crunch, he landed flat on his back, the ceiling spinning above him.

The Baggage Handler offered his hand. "May I help you up?"

Michael accepted the assistance and stood, rubbing his head. "Sorry. I must have tripped on the rug." He walked back to his suitcase and again tried to pick it up, but it was rooted to the spot. He stood back, perplexed. "That's not my suitcase, is it?"

The Baggage Handler tipped his cap. "You're welcome to check the baggage tags and the barcode on the side."

Michael checked the suitcase and felt a wave of relief; he wouldn't need to explain to his father that he'd lost his cherished baggage tags. He again grabbed the handle, gingerly this time, and tried to lift the suitcase. It was going nowhere.

"Why can't I pick it up?"

"Well, why don't you check? Open it."

Michael eyed it again, his hip throbbing from a lesson learned. He nudged the suitcase with a finger. This time it rocked. Just a gentle rock. Michael's eyes widened as the suitcase picked up momentum, rocking from side to side under its own steam. Michael backed away as it rocked back and forth more and more violently—until it reached its tipping point and crashed to the floor.

Michael gaped as the vibrations shot through his shoes. "What was that?"

The Baggage Handler gave a single nod. "It's okay. It's heavy."

Heavy? Michael squatted down next to the suitcase and gave it a nudge with his finger. It wasn't moving. He looked up to the Baggage Handler for approval.

Another single nod.

Michael gingerly grabbed the zipper in two fingers, and with slow clicks, he opened it. Taking a deep breath, he threw back the lid and reached in, expecting to see his running spikes. Instead, sitting on top of his design portfolio was a swathe of red participation ribbons and a sports trophy—a tiny golden plastic figure caught midstride.

Michael looked up at the Baggage Handler. "This isn't my stuff."

The Baggage Handler moved past him and sat on the sofa. He laced his fingers behind his head. "It's your baggage. You checked the tags. You checked the barcode."

Words of protest again swirled through Michael's mind, but as was their custom, they didn't come out of his mouth. "But . . . these aren't mine."

The Baggage Handler picked up the design portfolio and flicked open the cover.

Michael started toward the sofa. "Hey! Don't! Those are very—"

"Good." The Baggage Handler thumbed his way through Michael's artwork. Each new drawing brought a small squeal of appreciation or a deep sigh of contentment. Music to a creative's ears. "In fact, they're beyond good; they're amazing. You might be the most talented artist I've ever met."

Michael stopped dead in his tracks, the compliment unfamiliar but welcome. "Um, thanks?"

"How long have you been drawing?" The Baggage Handler turned another page to find a penciled self-portrait of Michael. "See, look at this one. The lines, the contrast . . . It's like a photograph."

Michael was torn. No one looked at his design portfolio. He'd been burned before by people who had handed it back to him with disinterest . . . or worse, advice. But this guy was getting what he was trying to do with his art.

The Baggage Handler turned another page with another sigh. "Oh wow. Look at this one. It's amazing!"

Michael shuffled his feet, uncomfortable with the praise coming his way, but craving more.

The Baggage Handler looked enthralled. He traced a finger over the face of Michael's mother as he looked up. "The sadness in her eyes, the despair. You express so much emotion through your art."

Competing thoughts clashed in Michael's head in raging combat. *He gets what I'm doing, but who is this guy?*

"Michael, why do you draw?"

The last time Michael had been asked that exact question was in high school art class; the only people to appreciate his talent were there. Whenever that question was asked at home, the word *draw* was always replaced with the word *bother*.

The Baggage Handler's finger slowed. "The fact you don't know what to say now would suggest you're not very good at expressing yourself other than through your art."

Michael blinked as he felt himself blush. His

emotions were best kept to himself, although he *had* learned to express them through the language of art. This Baggage Handler, who had known him for all of five minutes, had summed him up as if he'd known him forever. Was his art teacher behind this?

"Do you dream of being an artist?" The Baggage Handler fixed him with clouded blue eyes, a look approaching wistfulness.

How did this guy know so much about him? About his dream? "Of course. Every day."

"So why aren't you pursuing that dream?"

Michael felt his face flush again. There was one answer here, but he couldn't force himself to say it. A more common phrase entered his thinking. "Remember: the future belongs to those who believe in their dreams."

"What does that mean?"

"Dad's been saying that for as long as I can remember."

The Baggage Handler's eyes narrowed. "What does he do for a living?"

"He works in hardware."

The Baggage Handler chuckled. "That's usually the way. Anyway, you're a talented artist, not a shelf stocker in hardware. And the correct quote is 'those who believe in *the beauty of* their dreams.' Wise words."

Michael yearned for this praise to continue, but it was shadowed by a matching discomfort. He wanted—no, needed—to get the conversation back on track. "Look, as much as I appreciate your comments, I need to get out of here. If I mess up this scholarship . . ." Tears pricked the corners of his eyes. "I can't leave here with someone else's stuff in my suitcase. Whose *is* this?"

The Baggage Handler looked up from the design portfolio. "Have a look." Then he went back to sighing in impressed amazement as he turned a new page.

Michael squatted next to his suitcase and picked up a participation ribbon with a white button that had floral script rewarding the recipient for simply turning up. The button was surrounded by a bright red rosette, and two thin strips of red trailed beneath it. They were known in his house as loser ribbons. Michael had brought home one of these ribbons in his first race as a seven-year-old, and his father had hit the roof, wanting more. Demanding more. The memory rapped lightly on the lid it had nailed down on his self-esteem many years ago. He reached in and grabbed a handful of the tiny buttons. The suitcase seemed full of them.

Michael offered them to the Baggage Handler. "I didn't put these in here."

The Baggage Handler looked up at him. "I know. You didn't." He returned to the portfolio with another exclamation of glee.

"You know?"

The Baggage Handler put down the portfolio. "You didn't put them in there, but you are carrying them around."

"What are you talking about? When I put my spikes into my bag this morning at the airport, these weren't in here."

"I've already said that."

Michael was totally nonplussed as he looked back into the suitcase. "And who put a trophy in here?"

The Baggage Handler folded his arms. "Have a look."

Michael picked it up. The plastic, gold-colored athlete ran proudly on top of a hefty faux marble tribute to someone else's achievement. He'd won many trophies over the years, but he'd never seen this one before.

The Baggage Handler leaned forward and fixed a gaze on him with clouded blue eyes, a look approaching wistfulness. "A name on there should tell you who put all this into your baggage."

Michael sighed heavily and held up the trophy.

There *was* a name on there.

He stopped breathing.

It was his father's.

The photograph trembled in Gillian's hand. She lifted her glasses in slow motion, and her family smiled again. She reached down and picked up the other photos. Her family home shone in the afternoon sun as her boys raced their bikes on the driveway. Her family room was now the scene of a delightful evening with the five of them cuddled up on the sofa to watch a movie. Her church group, Gillian included, threw back their heads and laughed over coffee.

These were photos to be kept.

These were memories to be treasured.

But she'd never seen them before.

Blinking, her mind on overload, Gillian lowered her glasses back onto the bridge of her nose. The photos went back to their original state. Misery. Loneliness. Neglect.

Gillian opened her mouth to speak, but the words wouldn't come. She lifted her glasses again and then lowered them. Lifted and then lowered. Scowling, smiling. Train wreck, cozy. Weeds, sunshine. Happiness, misery. Togetherness, solitude. Contentment, neglect.

She took off her glasses and inspected the lenses. She held them up to the light. They were clear, as they always were.

She held up the glasses to the Baggage Handler, her thoughts exploding in a thousand directions at once. "There must be something wrong with these."

The Baggage Handler sat down and threw an arm across the sofa. He pointed to the far wall. "Who is quoted on that poster?"

Gillian repositioned her glasses and zeroed in on the caption below the sunflower. "Miranda Kerr. Why?" She again removed her glasses and held them at arm's length, as if they were contaminated.

"Well, there's nothing wrong with your glasses. You could read her name."

"But when I look at the photos with them on . . . I have to wear these. I can't see much without them."

The Baggage Handler smiled. "I suggest you can't see much *with* them either."

Gillian flicked through the photos and alternated between glasses on and glasses off. "How are you doing this?"

"I'm not doing this, Gillian. You are."

"What do you mean I'm doing it?"

The Baggage Handler cocked his head. "A buildup on them keeps you from seeing the world as it is."

Gillian waved her glasses at this strange young man. "Buildup? There's nothing on them."

The Baggage Handler smiled again. "I'm not

talking about dirt or grime. I'm talking about envy and comparison. You're looking at your world through distorted lenses. It's how you've come to see life."

Gillian folded her arms in defense, her glasses dangling from one hand.

The Baggage Handler fixed a gaze on her with clouded blue eyes, a look approaching wistfulness. "Look, you're not the only one who does this. I've seen it time and time and time again. A whisper is in the back of everyone's mind. You know it's there, and you can feel it. It asks you one simple, infuriating question: *How am I doing?* So you look around and measure yourself against everyone else."

The Baggage Handler had zeroed in on Gillian's greatest weakness: how she saw herself.

"It becomes a problem when you start to look at your own life while listening to that whisper more than anything else. It condemns you, and you now see your life, your family, your job, and your home in terms of disappointment, not value. You end up changing how you see your entire world."

Images flashed across Gillian's memory. The car that broke down so often she hated driving it. The family holiday that was never exotic enough. The house she found too embarrassing to invite new friends to. The boys she often apologized for. The husband who wasn't the cook Susanna's

130

husband was, the mechanic Vicki's husband was, or the breadwinner Debbi's husband was. The too few number of friends. The clothes always three seasons behind everyone else's. The figure she cloaked at the beach.

Gillian sank back into the sofa as the gravity of the Baggage Handler's revelation fell on her. He was right. She had come to measure her life by what she didn't have. What she wasn't. Who she wasn't. "Who are you? Even though you're in a Baggage Services cap and overalls, you don't work for the airline, do you? Are you some kind of guardian angel?"

"It's perhaps best if you just think of me as the Baggage Handler. I help people with their baggage—those who want to be helped, anyway!" A sadness filled his eyes. "Not everyone wants to be helped."

"Why don't people want to be helped?"

The Baggage Handler stared past Gillian, the sadness now flickering across his face. He gave a deep sigh. "Because dealing with baggage is hard. It requires effort or swallowing pride. Because some people are so used to carrying their baggage they don't think they can exist without it. Because some people say they need time to deal with it, but that time never arrives. But overall, for most people, it's because carrying baggage is just easier, despite the weight."

Gillian looked at the mirror facedown on her cocktail dress. "That's just sad."

"It's also quite normal. In fact, you're doing it right now."

Gillian shot a rapid-fire upward glance at him. "What do you mean?"

"We've talked for five minutes, but you haven't yet asked to be helped. You want to know about everything around your baggage, but you haven't asked how you can deal with it."

Gillian folded her arms and sat back on the sofa, putting some distance between herself and this strange young man.

"How did these photos get in here? I was the only one who packed this suitcase."

The Baggage Handler leaned forward, elbows on knees, and gently shook his head. "Oh no, Gillian, these are always in your baggage. They must drain you of energy when you have to lug them around all the time."

"Are you saying my family is happy when I'm not looking at them?"

The Baggage Handler chuckled. "I think you've missed the point. You've chosen to see your family through these lenses. When you do, you see them as miserable. That's the choice you've made."

"What do you mean it's a choice? I didn't know these items were in here until five minutes ago!"

The Baggage Handler held out his hands, and

Gillian handed over her glasses. He squinted through them.

"Your vision of everything around you is flawed. You choose to see your family through the lens of comparison. You measure them against everyone else, all the time, and that means you tend to see the worst in them. Not because of anything they've done or the people they are, but because of what they haven't done or who they aren't."

Gillian teared up as these observations sank into her soul. Thoughts she had worked hard to bury were suddenly brought into the light.

"You constantly choose to see your world through the eyes of someone who wishes life were better, that life were different."

Gillian wanted to argue, to stand up for herself, but her resolve evaporated because she knew, deep down, that the Baggage Handler was right.

He reached for the mirror. "Gillian, you live in a world today where you're told every part of your life isn't good enough. You've fallen for that. It's not a truth that will make your life better; it's a lie designed to keep you wanting more and buying more. It keeps the whole system running. But it's not good for you as a mom, as a wife, as a woman, or as a person."

"Everyone else does this as well, don't they?"

The slightest of smiles peered through the fog of the Baggage Handler's mood. "Everyone else says that too. But that's also based in comparison." The young man shifted on the sofa and crossed his legs. "Sure, your life isn't perfect, but it's also not as bad as you perceive it to be. Life isn't about what you've got. It's about what you do with what you've got. Let me tell you something few people know: every time you point at someone else and wish you were them, you're presuming they're happy and content. You're presuming that what you're seeing is what the other person is. That's not the case. You see, those people you wish you were like often look at others and wish they were someone else too."

The Baggage Handler shook his head. "I've seen this thousands and thousands of times. You're comparing your weaknesses to other people's strengths. You're comparing the parts of yourself you dislike to others' unique gifts. You focus on your dirty laundry and hold it up to their Sunday best."

Gillian knew she'd been like that for as long as she could remember—ever since her parents focused all their energy on their beautiful, overachieving, eldest daughter, Becky. A tiny crack appeared in her emotional tank, and tears once again welled in her eyes.

The Baggage Handler offered her a handkerchief. "Things aren't always what they seem, Gillian." He grabbed a banana from the fruit bowl and inspected it. "You see, it looks beautiful from a distance, but when you get up close and engage with it, you see it's not quite what it seems." He handed the banana to her.

The fake sheen of the plastic was light under her fingers, but the Baggage Handler gestured for her to push her glasses up onto her forehead. When she did, she saw the banana peel was dotted with black.

The Baggage Handler leaned into her suitcase, picked up the family photo, and sat on the sofa next to Gillian. "It's the same with your family." He pointed to her cross-eyed eldest son with his tongue poking out. "Tyson is a feisty little tyke, but he'll need that when he's older and stands up for the little guy. He'll make a career out of advocating for people without a voice. But you constantly wish he would be quiet." He pointed to the twins, one in a headlock. "You see James and Alex as fighting all the time. They won't be the best they can be without that fight, yet you want them to calm down."

Gillian's brain fogged. Calm and quiet were exactly what she wanted from her three boys. Those were the words she shouted over her shoulder into the back seat of the car during just about any trip they made.

The Baggage Handler picked up the other photos. "Look at your house. Sure, it's not perfect, but it's a home. Yet you look at it through the lens of what your sister has. Yes, she's just moved into this massive house, but do you know how much they've had to mortgage their future just to keep up with the other families in their social orbit?"

Gillian shook her head.

"No, you don't, because you've never asked. And even if you did, Becky wouldn't tell you. You just assume what Becky has is better than what you have."

Gillian's tears trailed down her cheeks.

"Do you know what else? You then decide what she has isn't just better than what you have but that what she has also makes her better than you."

The tears flowed freely now. This young man—this Baggage Handler—was looking deep into her soul and sticking his finger into every open wound.

"Gillian, you're playing a game you've already decided you've lost. And your family would like for you to stop playing." He put his hand on her arm. "I would like you to stop playing."

Rejection and decades of self-worthlessness cascaded out as her emotional tank cracked open, and Gillian broke down.

She looked up through the tears at the Baggage Handler, who himself was weeping. "What can I do? I don't want to be like this."

The Baggage Handler's eyes sparkled with

136

compassion. "I don't want you to be like this either."

"All right," Gillian said, sobbing. "How do I fix that?"

"I can clean your glasses for you." The Baggage Handler pulled out a rust-colored rag from the top pocket of his overalls. As he polished first one lens and then the next in slow, deliberate circles, he whistled a tune Gillian was sure she knew.

Gillian's sense of herself, crushed for so long under the boots of others, peeked out from under the oppression she had sentenced it.

The Baggage Handler looked at her through each lens and then smiled as he handed the glasses back to Gillian.

She put them back on and again looked at the photos. Her family was now smiling and cheeky. The boys powered their bikes down the driveway. Her church group laughed in one another's company, heads thrown back and smiles all round. Gillian lifted her glasses. The photos stayed the same.

The Baggage Handler waved his hand around the room. "Is anything else different?"

The waiting room had transformed. The white walls were scuffed. The TV picture was slightly fuzzy, pixels flashing out of sync across the screen. The posters had tattered edges. What was perfect before was now run-of-the-mill, verging on disappointing. It was normal. Gillian looked down at the fruit. The banana was black-spotted, and the apples were no longer waxy perfection. She gingerly picked one up and examined it. It was slightly discolored and had an ever-so-small bruise on one side.

The Baggage Handler nudged her. "Try it."

Gillian took a small bite, and her mouth was filled with sweet juice. It was the juiciest apple she'd ever tried. Another bite produced an enormous, satisfying crunch. She held it up. "When I looked at this apple before, it was fake."

"That was because that was how you were seeing things, Gillian. Now you're seeing it like it really is. It has its imperfections, but what do you think of the taste?"

Gillian took another bite. "I can't remember eating an apple so fresh."

The Baggage Handler leaned in. "Here's the thing: that apple always was tasty and fresh."

Gillian wiped away tears as she crunched on the delicious apple. "Thank you so much—whoever you are—for helping me deal with this." She placed the partially eaten apple on the coffee table and stood. "I'm going to be so much happier now that we've met."

She reached for her suitcase, but the Baggage Handler stopped her with a hand.

"We're not done yet."

—21—

David's insides seethed with a cocktail of anger and fear. He raised a quivering finger. "Where did you get this?"

The Baggage Handler sat back on the sofa, a picture of innocent calm as he crossed his legs. "Why do you assume I put it in there? You packed your bag. You carried it around. You locked it, and you opened it."

"Is this some kind of sick joke?"

"Well, I think so, and I think you should be angry with the person inflicting this on you."

David felt heat rising to his face as he folded his arms. "Finally, we're on the same page. Give me a name."

The Baggage Handler's eyebrows knitted together in surprise. "Well . . . you, David."

David's brain asked a thousand questions at once. He had no idea what to do with any of them. "Just . . . what . . ." Words, David's usual weapon of choice, deserted him. "Who are you?"

"I'm the Baggage Handler."

David huffed his impatience through clenched teeth. "No, who are you *really?*"

"Sorry, maybe I should speak a little slower for you. I . . . am . . . the . . . Baggage . . . Handler."

He chuckled, impressed at his own joke, and thick black curls sprung free as he scratched under his cap.

David lurched forward as if he were going to grab this young guy by the straps of his overalls. "Look, buddy, I've got no idea what's going on here, but I haven't got the time to work out if this is the most elaborate prank in history or if you're a stalker or whoever—whatever—you are. I need to get out of here. Show me the way out."

The Baggage Handler frowned as he studied his hands. "I'm afraid I can't do that. You promised to deal with your baggage before you left here today."

David clenched and unclenched his hands as the adrenalin surged through him like a rising tide. "Promised? What are you talking about?"

The Baggage Handler reached across to the counter, where he'd placed his clipboard. He turned it around and tapped his finger on the form David signed.

David stepped forward to read it. " 'I promise to make a choice about my baggage before I leave this facility.' " And then, at the bottom of the form, his hastily scrawled signature.

"It looks like you've got a choice to make." The Baggage Handler placed the clipboard next to him.

A white-hot rage flamed in the very fiber of David's being. He glared at the Baggage Handler, and then he stormed out of the room, only to be confronted once again by a line of white doors in a corridor disappearing into infinity. His ragged breathing caught in his throat and bounced into the distance. Trapped. He skulked back into the waiting room.

"Why me?" David stood at his full height. He had to wrestle back some power. Somehow.

"Why not?" The Baggage Handler laced his fingers behind his head.

Another escape route cut off. "All right, so I have to get out of here, and I have to make some kind of decision about all this stuff that has magically appeared in my suitcase. What do I have to do?"

The Baggage Handler gave a sage nod. "That's better. When did this thing happen with Sharon?"

David narrowed his eyes again. How did he know about that? Maybe Sharon was behind all this. Now *that* made sense. *Tread carefully.* "Last year."

"You've been carrying it around for six months, then, maybe longer."

A silence grew in the room, and then David waved a finger at the Baggage Handler as his careful tread disappeared under the adrenalin of indignance. "Hang on a minute. *She* cheated on *me,* so why do I have to deal with it? Why is it in my baggage?"

The Baggage Handler shrugged. "I've seen

this happen thousands of times. This isn't the baggage of someone who's been unfaithful. It's the baggage of unforgiveness."

"Unforgiveness?" David spat out the word.

"Yes, unforgiveness. You carry the consequences of someone else's behavior, and it ends up eating you alive. David, you're the one carrying your baggage around, and it's weighing you down. But you're choosing what to carry."

David simply stared. "That just shows you've read that newspaper."

"Read it, seen it, heard it, felt it, lived it. I've spoken to so many people in your situation, and the one thing you all have in common is holding on to bitterness because you think you're punishing the other person. But you end up paying the price yourself."

David dropped his head.

"I'm going to guess that you're angry, no fun to be around, resenting the world around you, and addicted to various things to self-medicate the pain. But then it gets worse. You can't sleep, and you live off antacids. Your body is drowning in bitterness. What you've done is drink poison in the hope that the person who wronged you will die."

David's eyes flitted back and forth as he processed these incisions into his life. This Baggage Handler was reading him like a book.

"And I've yet to meet a person who carries this

extra baggage and is either happy to carry it or doesn't feel its weight. And yet they still carry it."

David looked up at the Baggage Handler with a steely glare, his lips pursed.

The Baggage Handler studied him with piercing blue eyes. From the end of the counter, the alarm clock ticked louder, its tinny counting of the seconds bouncing off white walls.

"Why do you think that is, David?"

The beginning of an answer half escaped David's lips before his mind had a chance to reel it back in. "Because I'm . . ."

"You know, don't you?" The Baggage Handler leaned forward in eager anticipation, rubbing his hands together as David arrived at the right answer. "You feel it as well. It's because, deep down, you know you're—"

"Right." David again dropped his head and stared at the fraying white carpet. "She was the one who was wrong."

The Baggage Handler shook his head. "She was, but that doesn't mean you're completely right. Why do people think that for them to be right, the other side must be one hundred percent wrong? Life is far more nuanced than that."

David glowered. "So I'm to blame here? Is that it?"

Another shake of the head. "You're contributing to this mess as well. She was in the wrong—I agree with you—but you're contributing to the lack of a solution."

Sharon's voice rang in his ears. *I'm so sorry, David . . . It was a once-off thing . . . I was lonely, and you weren't listening.* Tears. Lots of tears. But none from David. Just the set of his jaw and a battle to keep his mind replaying the scene that led to the photo he found.

David's eyes softened a touch. "She thought it would be enough to say she was sorry."

"She *was* sorry. What did you do with that?"

"If I was to censor it and take out all the bad language?"

The Baggage Handler chuckled softly. "That would be nice."

"Then I didn't say much."

The Baggage Handler pointed at David's suitcase. "You're about to break up a family, devastate your daughter, and complicate your life because, deep down, being right is the most important thing to you."

"Look. Whoever you are—whatever you are— it's been a tough year, but I'm not the one who started all this."

A shadow passed over the Baggage Handler's eyes. "I know, but relationships don't break up one day out of the blue."

That sinking feeling was back in the pit of David's stomach. That sense of foreboding, of ownership. Of making a mistake.

"You're angry with her—obviously—but the question here isn't about what. It's about why."

Why? It was the smallest of questions, but it jolted David. It was a question he'd never allowed to be part of the argument that raged in his head. He had fought through the *who* and spent a lot of time fighting off the details of the *what*. But *why* was never invited into the discussion.

The Baggage Handler stood and smoothed his overalls. "This is a lot to take in, so I'll leave you for a few minutes to think about it. But just a reminder, you signed a form that said you would choose what to do with your baggage before you left, and the clock appears to be ticking toward your meeting." He moved to the door and turned the handle. "I'll be right back."

David sat down on the edge of the sofa, his knee keeping time with his machine-gun heartbeat as the alarm clock continued its tinny ticking. He stared at the photo in the suitcase, the image of his wife kissing his best friend flaming into life from slow-burning embers deep within him. His breathing grew shallower as his mind ticked over. He checked his phone. Another fifteen minutes gone. In forty-five minutes his career would be over.

It's why.

Sharon's voice again pierced his memory. *You're never home . . . I'm tired of eating dinner alone . . . You missed another recital, but it was so good to see Jerry there.*

A small crack appeared in his anger, a wall that he'd bricked in with the mortar of justified righteousness since he'd found the photo on her phone.

He hadn't wanted to work from dawn to dusk. No one did. But when you were the breadwinner and providing for a family that constantly needed you to provide, you did. For the clothes. The dresses. The endless carousel of princess movies.

Everything to make them happy.

The gnawing in the pit of his stomach grabbed him, but it didn't need an antacid. It needed something far deeper.

It's why.

With a downward glance, he made a connection that swept all his thoughts aside.

He had seen that polo shirt on the golf course several times.

And it was in the photo. Jerry had been wearing it on the ferry.

With his wife, whom he was kissing.

David leaned forward and picked up the photo. Sharon's lips shone a bright pink. His eyes shot to the collar on the shirt in the suitcase and the pink mark his wife's lips had left on it.

David screamed as he grabbed the tickets and receipts and tore them into strips until they were strewn all over the floor. He ripped the photo into confetti and took Jerry's shirt, pushing aside the twenty-year friendship with his best friend as the anger rose in him, and tried to rip it into shreds. He made a small tear and then a satisfying rip as the anger drove him to a frenzy. With an anguished scream he threw it in the trash can under the coffee machine. He slammed the suitcase shut and then sat back down on the sofa in triumph. "Right. Dealt with."

The insanity of the whole situation threatened to tip him upside down. David stood, his breathing ragged and his pulse racing. He needed to center himself and get back on track. He took the first steps on his usual journey to rationalize the whole experience. This had to be stress from the fight to save his career.

He closed his eyes and massaged his temples. "Right. I've dealt with whatever this sideshow is, and I've got to get back to this meeting. I need to think about my presentation."

He closed his eyes and tried to picture Caitlin on the ferry. She was smiling, but next to Sharon was someone else. Jerry now sat in his place.

David snapped his eyes open and trailed his fingertips in ever-faster hypnotizing circles on his temples. "Okay, I've got the reports." He needed to touch base with something in the real world, and an overwhelming desire to check the one thing that would save his career flared in his head.

He opened his eyes, but the usual feeling of calm wasn't quite back. This was different than it normally was when he nailed the lid on any situation getting away from him. One corner was loose, and he knew it.

The alarm clock's tinny ticks boomed across the room.

David opened the suitcase again. Sitting on top of the financial reports were a man's shirt with a lipstick stain, two ferry tickets, a couple of restaurant receipts, and a selfie of his wife kissing his former best friend.

22

Michael stared at the trophy, and time slowed as the seconds dripped into the pools of thought rippling in his mind. His fingers ran over the tiny figure. The engraving pulsed on the burnished gold surface, and he traced his finger across his father's name. And the name below it: Serviceton High School.

This trophy was Dad's? Michael racked his mind for some—any—kind of memory of seeing it on the mantelpiece between his brother's haul of glory and his own.

He drew a blank.

Then a second and third thought pressed in on him. *Why am I carrying this around? And why would Dad put it in my suitcase?*

From the sofa, the Baggage Handler quietly whistled. What was that tune? Michael knew it, but it crouched in a dark corner of his mind.

Michael offered the trophy to him. "Why would he do this?"

The Baggage Handler leaned back with a low whistle. "Why would who do what?"

"Dad. Put this trophy in my suitcase."

"I prefer to call it baggage."

Michael's anger flickered, and he poked a nervous head out from behind his usual defenses. Who cared what it was called?

The Baggage Handler smiled. "You've never seen this trophy, have you?"

Michael pulled back his hand. How did he know that?

"Do you know why you've never seen this trophy?"

Michael shook his head, his curiosity piqued.

"Because your father never wanted you to see it."

"How do you know that?"

The Baggage Handler fixed piercing blue eyes on Michael. "You'd be surprised."

Michael folded his arms, still grasping the trophy. "Really? Try me."

The Baggage Handler moved from the sofa and squatted down next to Michael. "Because I've seen this thousands of times, even down to a similar athlete on the top of the trophy. And the reason is *always* the same. Michael, your father is a proud man. He obviously thought if you saw this, it would change how you felt about him."

Michael ran his fingers over the golden figure. His father had talked for years about how he could have been an Olympian but never had the opportunity. "How would this change how I felt about him? So he won some trophies. So did I."

The Baggage Handler smiled, yet he looked a bit sad. "Because it made him feel inferior, he thought you'd see him as inferior."

Inferior? Michael again stared at his father's

name, etched in a flowing script on the plaque on the marble column. The harsh fluorescent light caught it, and the plaque began to glow. A flash of light spread across it, and then a gray patch extended into a line and then a second and a third to complete the letter. Michael was transfixed as two more words were added to the plaque.

Eighth place.

Michael knew what that meant in a race of eight runners.

"But my father never tried athletics."

"I think you'll find he did, Michael."

"So why would he put this in my baggage?"

"We'll get to that." The Baggage Handler nodded at the suitcase.

Michael again looked inside. The sea of red rosettes had parted to reveal paper underneath. Michael swept the ribbons aside to reveal dozens of participation certificates, each labeled with his father's name and the bulk-printed logo of Serviceton High School. They looked like the artistic merit certificates he had brought home every year he was in school. Certificates that divided his parents—his mother's encouragement was often tempered with his father's comments about the poor prospects of an artistic career.

But these weren't certificates of merit. He shuffled through them—participation in the 400m, participation in the 1500m. Tried hard in the 110m hurdles. Participated in cross-country but didn't finish. His father had tried everything. And failed.

Michael made his way to the sofa, realization shining into every dark corner of his childhood. "Is this real?" He let go, and the certificates fluttered back into the suitcase.

"This is very real. You've carried this baggage all the way here."

Michael dropped onto the sofa, fireworks bursting in his head. The fake timber of the chunky TV, the explosion of color, the mismatched furniture, the rickety mustard-yellow fridge. Old trophies he'd never seen before. Certificates from his father's failed attempts to be an athlete.

This strange guy.

"Where is here?"

The Baggage Handler tapped the badge on his overalls. "This is Baggage Services! This is where people come to deal with their baggage."

"Are you part of the airline?"

The Baggage Handler laughed. "No."

Michael tried to put this experience in some kind of order, some sort of sense. It hurt his head. "How can you not be a part of the airline but have my suitcase?"

"We prefer to call it baggage."

"How did I get the wrong baggage?"

Silence. The hint of a smile under a navy-blue cap.

Michael mentally retraced his steps at the airport. "I grabbed it off the carousel—"

Silence. Michael connected the dots.

"—without looking." The last dot connected to the others.

The Baggage Handler clicked his fingers. "Bingo! In fact, you all did."

You all? "How many other people are here?"

"You'd be surprised."

"Who knows about this place?"

The Baggage Handler yawned in an extravagant stretch. "Everyone."

"So that suitcase I brought in. That was someone else's baggage? Did you give it to them? What are they doing?"

The Baggage Handler's brow furrowed. "They're dealing with it, in their own way."

"What does that mean?"

The Baggage Handler leaned forward. "Why are you interested in people you've never met? You all want to know how everyone else is handling their own baggage, almost as an excuse to not deal with your own. Dealing with your baggage is hard. Carrying it appears to be easier, but it's not, and it can destroy people in the long run." The Baggage Handler bit his lip as if holding back tears. "And you've asked me about someone else, not how you can deal with your own baggage."

Michael fought back his own tears as he lifted

his father's certificate from the suitcase. Tears of shock. Anger. Frustration. "He always said I wasn't good enough, except when I was winning a race. Even then he'd ask me if I could shave another tenth off my time."

The Baggage Handler fixed a gaze on him with clouded blue eyes, a look approaching wistfulness. "I think you can see who he was disappointed in."

In that moment Michael understood. He wasn't carrying around his father's disappointment in him. He was carrying around his father's disappointment in himself.

The Baggage Handler picked up the school trophy. "Eighth place. Your father decided that rather than dealing with all his baggage about his failure, he would get you to carry it. That's completely unfair to you—and I can't express just how sorry I am he did that—but you don't have to carry it."

Tears blurred the room. "It would make sense that his stuff would end up in my baggage and not Scott's." Living in the shadow of an older brother who played his father's beloved ball sports had stunted Michael's growth for as long as he could remember.

The Baggage Handler smoothed his overalls, compassion sparkling in his eyes. "In Scott's baggage is exactly what you're carrying here. I'll have a conversation with him once his baggage gets too heavy for him as well. Michael, your father's baggage is taking up precious space in your own life, and it's weighing you down."

The weight of years of rejection perched squarely on Michael's shoulders. He stared at the carpet.

"If Dad's baggage is taking up space in my life, why have I carried it?"

"An excellent question that's difficult to answer. It's partially because you didn't realize it was there. Look, the problem isn't you've been handed some baggage. Everyone has baggage. It's that it's difficult for you to move forward with your life. Every time an opportunity presents itself, you can't move quickly because this weight drags behind you."

The Baggage Handler nodded, a single tear streaking its way down his face. "That's been there for a very long time. A very long time. I'm sorry about what has happened with your father. You've heard how you can pick your friends but you can't pick your family? That's true for you. But you *don't* need to carry this baggage. You have a choice."

Well, that's good news. I don't have to carry it.

But the next thought was terrifying. "Do I have to give all this back to my dad?" His father was a hard man to deal with in the best of times. The conversation about messing up the meeting with Coach Crosswell would be difficult enough.

Handing back this trophy and the certificates would be impossible.

"No, you can leave it all with me."

Michael shook his head in amazement. "Who *are* you?"

The young man simply tipped his cap, and black, curly hair sprung free over his forehead. "I'm the Baggage Handler. I'm here to help you with your baggage."

Michael sighed as he checked his phone. "What's the point? I've missed the rest of my meeting with the coach because of my baggage."

The Baggage Handler chuckled. "You were going to miss out on that scholarship because of your baggage anyway. And it's not pointless."

"What do you mean?"

"Apart from the fact that if you deal with your baggage today, you won't need to carry it around with you for the rest of your life, what if I were to tell you there's another way to achieve your dream? Not your father's. Yours."

23

David cradled his head in his hands as he rocked back and forth on the sofa. His anger was gone, shoved out of the way by a feeling that had threatened to mug him for six months. A feeling he had found impossible to banish without the constant presence of his anger.

He had brought this on.

A single sob rose in his throat, and he forced it back down with the little composure he had left. The door opened, and the Baggage Handler looked at the confetti on the floor and shook his head. "I'm amazed at how many people think that's the best way to deal with their baggage."

David looked through tears that were foreign to him. "Why is this happening?"

The young man sat down next to him. "Because you're carrying around baggage that's more than weighing you down. It's killing you. Literally. I've seen it all before—I'm guessing digestion problems, headaches, sleepless nights?" He counted them off on his fingers.

David stared at the floor as the Baggage Handler ticked off his health problems as though he were reading down a menu.

The Baggage Handler leaned into him. "And

that's not to mention what's happening to your heart."

Fear gripped David with an icy hand. "What do you know about my heart?"

The Baggage Handler fixed a gaze on him with clouded blue eyes, a look approaching wistfulness. "More than you'll ever know."

David sniffed back control, avoided the young man's sad eyes, and cleared his throat. "Why am I the one who has to deal with this?"

The Baggage Handler put out his hands. "You've been hurt. You've been betrayed. But your baggage isn't the betrayal. You've been using it to justify other things you're doing."

David narrowed his eyes as he folded his arms. "Such as?"

"For one, you've used it to justify hurting Sharon for months. That trip a few months ago, at the karaoke bar when those girls—"

David's mouth fell open. "You know about that?"

"Of course. And you thought staying angry justified doing it. Good for the goose, good for the gander, and all that."

David's mind raced. This guy was picking out his flaws with surgical precision.

"I know about all things, including the ultimatum you gave to your wife last night."

David's neck threatened to snap as he spun to face the Baggage Handler.

"But she and Jerry—"

"I know. As I said, you have a right to feel betrayed, but you're responsible for your behavior, not hers."

The injustice again raged inside David. "I've nearly killed myself to provide for my family. I get repaid like that, but it's *my* problem?"

The Baggage Handler nodded.

"Everything I did—all the work I put in, all the extra hours—I did to make them happy."

Still that slow nod.

"She tells me she doesn't want me to work so much, but we never seem to have enough money—"

"David, your marriage has been in trouble for longer than six months. You've got to understand that you've contributed to that, and when Sharon—"

"Now, hang on a minute—"

The Baggage Handler again put out his hands. "I'm not saying you're wrong. Your wife shouldn't have done what she did. My heart breaks for what happened to you, and I don't condone the way she chose to handle the distance between you. I'm glad she's tried to own what she did, but I've seen this time and time again. When people come here carrying unforgiveness, they feel like they've got a Get Out of Jail Free card because of what's been done to them. And in the past six months, you've been looking for evidence she's still having an affair behind your back. Checking her phone for more photos. Working out if she's got email accounts you don't know about."

David stopped breathing. That was *exactly* what he'd been doing.

"You haven't found anything, have you?"

He hadn't.

"That's because, as she said, it was over, but the part of you that was hurt almost needed to believe it was still going on."

David's breath came back. Slow. Fuming.

The Baggage Handler leaned back and crossed his ankles.

"But still you look. Here's my question: how is that working out for you?"

A numbness spread down David's spine and froze every joint. The Baggage Handler was right. It *wasn't* working out for him. As much as it was making him feel righteous, it was making his marriage—and, in turn, his life—worse.

"Your digestion is shot to bits, and the headaches . . . Do you think there's a chance that's all linked?"

"Listen here—"

"When did the stomach trouble start?"

David reined in the answer before it shot out of his mouth. It was six months ago. When his suspicions had driven him to sneak a peek at

Sharon's phone while she was in the shower, and he found the photo.

"Have you never wondered why?"

No, he hadn't.

"And then you've got the situation at work. Have you been a good boss in the past few months?"

The cinema of David's memory now flashed with the faces of those members of his team who left after yet another one of his explosions—the good salespeople, the ones responsible for their record-breaking year. And the ones they'd left behind were the deadwood, the serial underperformers who knew they would never get a job anywhere else.

The Baggage Handler leaned forward into a conspiratorial crouch with David. "This is all because you refuse to forgive her."

David stared hard at the floor, unable to look at this man who was staring into his soul with x-ray vision.

"What do you mean? I didn't even know all this was in here until thirty minutes ago."

"Well, now you do, and now you've got a decision to make."

David stared into the open suitcase. Jerry's polo shirt. The photo. Somehow reassembled. He pursed his lips. "And what about her?"

The Baggage Handler smiled. "You weren't listening. She's responsible for her behavior.

There will be a time when Sharon and I have a conversation she won't want to have, and she will face the way she hurt you. But that doesn't let you off the hook for dealing with your baggage now."

A resolve hardened in David. Sharon wouldn't get off scot-free. Good. "I can't tear this up or throw it in the trash. What are my choices?"

"It's quite simple. You can choose to keep carrying your baggage, or you can leave it with me."

"I can't leave my suitcase with you; it's got all the financial reports—"

The Baggage Handler shook his head with a soft chuckle. "Why are you not getting this? And stop calling it a suitcase. It's baggage. You have a simple decision to make. Leave your baggage with me or keep carrying it."

Leaving behind the baggage would be so simple. This guy was right, and what David was doing wasn't working. All he had to do was reach into the suitcase . . .

He glanced down at the polo shirt and the photo. His wife, full of the joy of the moment, smiling and carefree. Happy. And with another man.

Tick. Tick. Tick. Tick.

The Baggage Handler folded his arms, and his voice took on a harder edge. "What's the real pain here, David? You're angry, but why?"

David's thoughts raced. It should be obvious,

but the words wouldn't come. He was angry because . . . He was angry because . . .

Tick. Tick. Tick. Tick.

The answer revealed itself in a moment of sheer clarity. The ticking of the alarm clock slowed, slowed, until it stopped. A single thought dropped unbidden into his head. He was angry because he knew he had contributed to their problem, even in a small way. In his drive to provide for his family, he had driven her away.

The Baggage Handler smiled. "I'm not saying you need to move on as if nothing happened. But you have taken an important first step toward making this decision."

The bile of injustice again rose and swept away his thoughts. "It shouldn't be my decision. She needs to pay for this. I'm the one who stayed faithful to my marriage vows." His voice cracked as it grew louder, and his fingers fanned out the restaurant receipts. "I might need these when I get back home."

The Baggage Handler's face darkened as his cell phone rang. "If you want to let your anger loose at someone responsible for all this, there's a mirror over there. That's where you need to start." He gestured to the far wall. "I'll give you another minute, and then I'll be back." He stood, smoothed his overalls, and whistled that maddeningly familiar tune as he left the waiting room.

Pressure and guilt pressed in on David from every side, pinning him to the sofa, his muscles frozen in place. Then the tune the Baggage Handler had been whistling revealed itself. For a father of a six-year-old girl obsessed with the characters from *Frozen*, it should have been tattooed on his brain, based on the number of times it had blared from the car stereo, a tiny girl's voice belting the lyrics from the back seat.

The Baggage Handler had been whistling "Let It Go."

David dropped his head, and the tears came again.

—24—

Gillian froze. "We're not done yet?"

The Baggage Handler nodded his head at the open suitcase. "We've dealt with how you see the rest of the world, and now we need to do something about how you see yourself."

Nerves slowed Gillian's faltering speech as she reached into the suitcase for the silver mirror. "O . . . kay."

It was gone. A mirror was there, but it wasn't silver. This one had a chunky, heavy, black frame.

"What happened to the silver mirror?"

"The mirror was never silver, Gillian. Now you're seeing the world for what it is. You're seeing the mirror for what it is. It was always like that."

Gillian wrapped shaky fingers around the thick handle, careful to keep the reflective side away from her as she turned it over. It was now wavy and distorted, like a carnival mirror. Old habits kicked in as she avoided catching her own gaze. But this fantastical mirror that was once silver—but was never silver—drew her in. She snuck a peek. Her hair was everywhere, and black bags underlined her eyes. Then it dawned on her. This was what she looked like in this mirror, but it was distorted.

Gillian held the mirror at arm's length. "I look no different."

"But now you know it's the mirror that's distorted." The Baggage Handler's eyes sparkled with compassion. "Why is it so hard for you to see yourself as you are? You don't think that's the real you?"

"How many people see themselves like this?"

"You're gear-shifting the subject, Gillian—a move you've perfected over the years. But the answer is, you'd be surprised. One of the big giveaways is when someone draws attention to themselves for the sole reason of eliciting praise from others for reassurance."

The air filled with heavy implication, and Gillian understood what he was talking about. Or, more specifically, about whom. "Becky."

"That's the thing. You've spent your whole life measuring yourself against your sister, and you've never realized that, as much as you want to be Becky, most of the time *she* doesn't even want to be Becky."

Gillian turned the mirror over in her hands. She looked again at her reflection, the scales falling from her eyes and her mind, inch by inch, realizing the mirror she used to see herself in was damaged. "Why do we do this to ourselves?"

"I don't think there's an easy answer. Maybe it's a primal drive of competition to survive. Maybe it's the slick marketing of the twenty-first century delivered by advertising sharks with two-hundred-dollar haircuts and Gucci loafers. But so many of you avoid seeing the real you."

Gillian sat back on the sofa, the question she had buried for years now scratching its way to the surface. "Who is the real me?"

The Baggage Handler pointed to the full-length, mahogany-framed mirror on the wall. "She's in there."

Gillian stiffened as a primal terror reached up from deep within and grabbed her by the throat. "I don't want to see the real me."

The Baggage Handler fixed a gaze on her with clouded blue eyes, a look approaching wistfulness. "Why not?"

The shadow of an answer flitted across her mind. It comforted and defined her, but it had also shackled her and become the answer she lived by. Her voice came in a whisper. "Because I'm not worth looking at."

A tear trickled its way down each of the Baggage Handler's cheeks. "You *are* worth looking at. You were made for a purpose; you have your mix of skills, talents, and personality traits for a reason. Comparison ignores what makes you, *you*. You shouldn't be someone else. You're Gillian." His voice rose with passion as he got to his feet. "Don't you see? That's your problem! You see others better than they are because of how you feel about yourself! It justifies this view." The Baggage Handler's voice dropped to an impassioned whisper. "But it's also not true."

Gillian's reflex was to brush him off, but the Baggage Handler wouldn't be denied as he reached out to her, trembling fingers spread wide.

"This has always been a problem for you—and it always will be—until you make a choice to change."

Defiance from decades of experience crept into Gillian's voice as she tried everything to push this conversation away. "But everyone *is* better than me."

The Baggage Handler stared off into the distance. "Who says what they present to the world is real? They're spending their lives wondering if they measure up to what everyone else is doing. Take Becky for example—"

Gillian huffed. "My sister is perfect. I *do* wish I was like her."

"Why?" The Baggage Handler threw out frustrated hands as he snapped his response.

Gillian jumped. Her inner monologue streamed out of her. "Well, she's gorgeous. She's rich because she's married to a guy who earns a heap of money . . ." The more she spoke, the easier the words tumbled out. "Her daughter is getting married. She has a lot of rich friends—"

The Baggage Handler cocked his head. "All

stuff she wants you to see. Have you ever asked how she's doing behind the mask?"

Over the phone, she and Becky had had several false starts toward genuine sharing, but the conversations always veered to the shallows. Her sister was gifted in glossing over anything real and moving on to topics in which she was fluent. Which were safe. "I've tried, but she moves the discussion on to what she's bought or what she's done."

The Baggage Handler stroked his chin. "And why do you think that is?"

The answer dawned on Gillian like the first crack of light at sunrise. She drifted back to the button her sister wore at the airport, the one about being the mother of the bride. Becky acted like she wasn't interested in attention, but she spent her life in a desperate attempt to be noticed.

The Baggage Handler knelt in front of Gillian. "May I give you an insight into your sister that might help?" His voice dropped to a whisper. "She's terrified anyone will see the real her."

"But Becky is some kind of superwoman—"

"That's what she wants you to think, but I've seen so many people who wear the cape not because it will help them fly, but so they can be identified as a hero."

The pieces of Becky's life fell into place like completing a jigsaw puzzle. Her constant talk of busyness. The car that had to be newer than everyone else's. A husband spoken of only in terms of his achievements.

"Plus," he said, "the cape is ideal to help them hide what they're carrying around."

That first crack of light now expanded into a wide beam. In an instant her sister made sense, and for the first time in a very long time, Gillian no longer looked up to her sister with awe.

"Anyway, enough about Becky," the young man said. "Back to you. What would Rick do if he was married to Becky?"

Gillian laughed. She and Rick had joked about that for years, and his answer was always the same. "He would disappear into his shed and never come out."

The Baggage Handler's piercing eyes sparkled. "Do you love Rick?"

Tears welled in Gillian's eyes. "With all my heart."

The Baggage Handler fixed a gaze on her with clouded blue eyes, a look approaching wistfulness. "So why do you want to be like someone who would chase away the man you love with all your heart?"

This insight illuminated the whole picture of her life, her sister, and her family. Light shone into the corners of Gillian's life she had kept dark for years. The iron grip of her self-esteem inched apart.

"Your family wants you to see the real you.

Rick wants you to see the real you. And I want you to see the real you." He stood and held out his hand.

Gillian stared past him at the full-length mirror on the wall. It was a few feet away, but it would require her to travel miles over emotional quicksand covered with thorns and bracken.

"What do you say, Gillian?"

Her self-loathing fought one last battle to convince her that a look in the mirror was the last thing she wanted to do, but she drew a deep breath and took the Baggage Handler's outstretched hand. It was warm.

He smiled at first, and then his face broke into a massive grin.

Gillian's jelly legs wobbled as she slowly took the few steps toward the mirror. She stood in front of it, her eyes glued to the carpet.

The Baggage Handler stood to one side, a small squeal escaping his lips. He drummed his fingertips against each other, faster and faster, like a child on Christmas morning at the top of the stairs.

With a deep breath, Gillian forced her eyes from the carpet up to the reflection of her feet. Her shoes were different, less scuffed. Her eyes made their way up until she caught her own gaze and was staring herself full in the face.

"Oh."

Michael's eyes flicked left and right. Another way? To be an artist? His mind tumbled through the possibilities before they were swallowed by a familiar heaviness that settled on him like a thick blanket. *What if I'm not up to it?*

The Baggage Handler gave a soft chuckle. "Why do you think you won't be up to it? You don't even know what that opportunity is."

Michael shot a look at this strange young man with the big grin. "How can you tell what I'm thinking?"

He tipped his cap. "Because I'm the Baggage Handler."

"Okay, it looks like that's your response for everything. What is this new opportunity?"

The Baggage Handler fixed a gaze on Michael with clouded blue eyes, a look approaching wistfulness. "Before we get to that, I think it's important to discuss why you don't think you'll be up to an opportunity you know nothing about."

Michael frowned and chewed his bottom lip. "Well . . . I guess it's . . ." The words jostled in his mind to find the right order, but they stayed on the starting grid.

The Baggage Handler leaned forward to

encourage a response from Michael. "Don't try to say the right words; just say it."

A pressure valve in Michael, stuck for years, popped, and an honest thought jumped unfiltered from his mouth. "Because I've heard my whole life how I'm not any good, so it must be true."

The phrase bounced around the room, its echo both assaulting and teasing Michael's ears. His spine tingled with the elation of the release of something that had been trapped within him forever, yet a numbness spread as, for the first time, he heard it out loud. The voice was free, but it was still in the same room as him.

The Baggage Handler fixed a piercing gaze on him, and then his eyes softened. "Wow, that's pretty harsh. But if you don't mind, I do need to say your artwork suggests otherwise."

The familiar reactions rushed forward as Michael went into autopilot and batted away the praise. "It's just art. It's not anything that's useful or that I can base a career on."

"Now you sound like your dad."

He was right. In Michael's head, those reactions always sneered at him in his dad's voice.

"May I ask you something, Michael? What does your father know about art?"

A light chuckle escaped Michael's lips. "Not much." He dropped into a near-perfect voice impression of his father. "You won't pay the bills with your pencils, son."

The Baggage Handler nodded and tapped a finger to his lips. "So he's not the best judge of your talent, is he?"

A single crack drove up the middle of the wall he had built around his self-belief to defend against his dad's constant rejection.

"You say your dad works in hardware."

"Yep."

"How long has he been working in that hardware store?"

"Too long. His words."

The Baggage Handler stroked his chin. "So why would you take career advice from a man who's so unhappy with the choices he's made?"

With that revelation, Michael sank into the sofa, stunned. This guy was right.

The Baggage Handler gestured at the open suitcase. "You've got to understand, the way you see your true self is through your dad's eyes. But that's because of how he saw himself. Every day he saw himself as a disappointment, and then when you came along, that was all he knew, so he transferred that to you."

Michael's voice crawled out of him in a whisper. "I always thought Dad didn't believe I was ever good enough."

The Baggage Handler's voice trembled as he pointed a quivering finger at Michael, his face reddening. "You mustn't believe that. It's because he never felt *he* was good enough, but now it's holding *you* back." He breathed deep and ragged.

The fear that usually rose within Michael in the presence of anger didn't come. Instead, he felt something else. A comfort. A sense of protection. Someone was standing up for him.

In an instant, the Baggage Handler's anger seemed to melt away, replaced by a gaze from clouded blue eyes, a look approaching wistfulness. "Do you still want to keep dragging that baggage everywhere, stopping you from taking the opportunities that come your way?"

"Well, no, but what can I do about it? Do I give this stuff to you?"

"Sure." The Baggage Handler gave a broad smile.

"And I don't need to give it to my dad at all?"

"No, I'll handle that, although if you're going to deal with this once and for all, you need to accept yourself for who you are."

Michael's eyes followed the Baggage Handler's lifted finger as he pointed to the poster on the wall. *You are you. Embrace it.*

"Okay, I get it." Michael nodded down at the open suitcase. "Take it."

"No." The Baggage Handler folded his arms.

Confusion exploded inside Michael's head. "Hang on a minute. You just said I could leave it—"

"That's not what I said at all. I said you need to

give it to me. There's a huge difference between that and asking me to take it."

Michael churned that one over. "That's just semantics."

The Baggage Handler leaned forward, elbows on his knees, his fingers laced. "Oh no, it's far more than that. This is what people don't understand. When you hand your baggage to me, it's a conscious act of your will to hand it over, and then"—he framed the room with his hands—"this is the most important part: when you give it to me, you need to let go of it."

Michael nodded. "Fair enough." He reached down into the suitcase and picked up the trophy. He looked at the plaque one final time and held it out to the Baggage Handler, who took it, a tear in his eye. Michael scooped up his father's ribbons and certificates and dropped them into the Baggage Handler's arms.

The tiniest weight lifted from Michael's shoulders—a release from the crushing pressure he'd adjusted to. Michael lifted his shoulders, free of gravity for the first time in forever.

"I feel . . . different."

But a heaviness flitted across the Baggage Handler's face. "We're not done." And he pointed again to the suitcase.

—26—

A fiery tempest raged in David's soul. His rational self fought hard as it stood on one inalienable fact. This setup—whatever it was—was crazy. His emotional self—so often the underdog—tiptoed forward and observed that this strange young man from Baggage Services had a point. He *had* been working too hard. He *hadn't* been around. While he was killing himself to provide everything his wife and child wanted to be happy, he hadn't provided the one thing they needed—him.

David closed his eyes as the battle raged on, and they snapped open as the victor announced itself. He had no choice. He had to do something, or else he would lose his family anyway once he lost his job.

His rational self was adamant in triumph. Baggage was simple. You packed it before a trip, unpacked it after a trip, put it in the closet until the next trip. He would deal with it and then pack it away. That was the only way out of here: hand over this stuff—however it got into his suitcase was a question for later—and get back to head office. David looked down at his suitcase, the decision clear. He would get this over with and be on his way. He nodded to himself. *Sorted.*

The Baggage Handler came back into the room, still whistling "Let It Go."

David prickled. "Hilarious."

The Baggage Handler cocked his head. "I thought it more relevant than funny. Anyway, what are you going to do?" Crystal-blue eyes beneath a thick curl bouncing across a forehead once again pierced deep into David's soul.

He checked his phone. Twenty minutes until his presentation. He could still make it.

"I've made my decision." David stood. "I tried tearing up everything and throwing it in the trash. I don't know how you people did this, but when I reopened my suitcase, that stuff was back. Great trick, real Penn and Teller–type stuff there."

The Baggage Handler frowned. "That was no trick. That happened because it wasn't a decision. It was avoidance. You can't throw this stuff away, forget it, and hope your situation will get better. I'm just thankful there wasn't a shovel left in here this time. The last guy tried to bury his baggage, and it popped right out of the ground. He almost fainted."

Nineteen minutes. "You've got a point. I have been working like a dog all year, so I can see how that might have contributed a little bit to our problems."

The Baggage Handler beamed. "I'm pleased you've started to realize that. I don't expect you to put everything behind you this minute; it will take time, and you deserve that time to heal. Forgiveness isn't easy, but you need to at least start. You'll need to give your baggage to me, and then—"

David dived into his suitcase and grabbed the items that in forty-five minutes had gone from nothing to the biggest stumbling block in his life. "Here, take it!"

The Baggage Handler moved past David and perched on the edge of the sofa as he stroked his chin. "I sense you're not sincere about this. Do you *really* want to deal with your baggage and move on?"

David pinched the bridge of his nose as his pulse pounded in his ears. Eighteen minutes. "You asked me to give this to you, and now I'm doing it. Of course I'm sincere."

The Baggage Handler folded his arms and cocked his head, studying David. He nodded, once.

"Handing over your baggage is just the start, but there's one way I'll know you're sincere."

David exhaled in growing frustration, his heart now pounding hard. "You said—"

The Baggage Handler stood and smoothed his overalls. "Yes, I said you needed to deal with your baggage. Let's deal with it once and for all, shall we?" He ushered David to the full-length mirror on the far wall.

What now? David stood in front of his

reflection, the polo shirt and photo crumpled in his fists.

The Baggage Handler leaned around David to talk to his reflection. "You might have heard the phrase 'forgive and forget.' Forgiveness is not just forgetting everything that happened. It's much more than that, but in some ways so much less."

The feet of David's reflection faded in the mirror, and a gray-and-white static replaced them. It spread across the mirror and swallowed him whole.

Shocked, David half turned to the Baggage Handler. "What—"

"Watch."

In the center of the mirror, a patch of angry, almost-black static softened to a light gray. The patch grew toward the top and bottom of the mirror into the outline of a person. Then the first color appeared at the bottom of this figure. Bright pink. Then flesh. Painted toenails poked through a woman's open-toed sandals.

David was transfixed as the gray morphed to shapely legs, covered by white linen pants.

A tingle started at the base of David's spine and crawled its way up to his neck. Those legs had won him over years ago. Above them was a teal-blue blouse David knew well, as recognizable as the day he bought it three years ago.

David gaped. "How—"

"Watch."

Sharon's face filled in, her long brunette curls bouncing on her shoulders. David was eye to eye with his wife. They stared at each other in quiet wonder. For the first time in a long time.

Sharon's reflection stared, as if studying him. She frowned, and tears welled in her eyes. She moved to speak, and a whisper drifted from the mirror in a trail of vapor.

"I'm so, so sorry."

David had heard those words before. A long time ago. They came with the same sincerity that had come with her first few apologies. The ones he'd stormed out on. Sharon's sincerity had faded since then.

The Baggage Handler's voice appeared at his shoulder. "She wants your forgiveness. Do you forgive her?"

The polo shirt in David's hand trembled as he stared, eroding the stone he'd created inside himself for protection. Still, he was safe behind it. "She crushed me. All that work was so I could provide for them—"

A single sob came from behind David. "I know . . . I know . . . But you need to let it go."

David's emotional side stormed forward, laying claim to ground he'd conceded. It reminded him he had wanted to move on, but something always stopped him. Always. Memories of past events he knew little about and imagination that painted detail in angry color. He looked down at his feet. The suitcase. The polo shirt with the bright pink lipstick stain. His indignance fought back for control.

"I can't. Everything I did to provide for her—"

Tears bubbled to the surface, further eroding the stone around his heart. He fought hard to push them down into the place he'd allocated for them. Deep down.

The Baggage Handler's voice now appeared to be floating above him. "Forgiveness is starting somewhere. Let's try it with a few simple words. Words you've kept down. Deep down."

But the words wouldn't rise. David's chest ached, and his stomach grabbed him. Again.

"What's done is done, David. But what isn't done is the pain you're causing yourself."

A crack appeared in his defenses, and a sliver of light shone through. The thought of forgiving his wife eased into his mind and then lingered as it wasn't banished. The pain in his chest eased. The knot in his stomach he'd grown accustomed to loosened.

A hand clamped on his shoulder and squeezed. "Let it go."

David squeezed his eyes shut, warmed by a glow in his chest he hadn't felt for years as life flowed through veins that had hardened under a thick treacle pulse of anger and bitterness.

"This is about trust, David. You can move

forward. You need to have many conversations with Sharon, but they won't start if you won't accept her."

David's indignance wrestled for control one last time and lost. "I think I do forgive her."

The warmth spread through him. He felt light on his feet as he opened his eyes. Tears ran down the cheeks of Sharon's reflection.

A hint of flint appeared in the Baggage Handler's voice. "Words are powerful. You *think* you do or really do?"

He could forgive her. It would take a while for him to trust her again, but he was willing to try.

Sharon's reflection smiled. The same crooked smile that captivated him across the restaurant ten years ago. The same crooked smile that said, *I do*. The same crooked smile he hadn't seen for six months.

The Baggage Handler's voice still carried a harsh edge. "To truly forgive is to move beyond the pain. And to trust."

David returned Sharon's smile for the first time in a long time. But as she smiled, her lips fizzled and crackled as they glowed and shone. They turned bright pink. The shade she saved for special occasions.

A splinter caught in David's mind.

Sharon's reflection flicked a glance down at David's hands and smiled.

David followed her eyes to the polo shirt he still held. The bright pink on the collar . . .

His anger whirred into action like a giant turbine awakened for power.

Sharon held his gaze. That crooked smile . . .

David's breathing shortened as the pain of betrayal rushed at him. His anger accelerated as a bitter distrust rose in his throat with bile he'd been used to choking back or treating with antacids.

I knew it wasn't over!

The smile fell from Sharon's face as she put out her hands, as if to say, *What more can I do?*

David closed his eyes as his temples throbbed with white-hot anger. The photo and polo shirt shook in his fists as a tremor worked its way up his arms.

The Baggage Handler's voice appeared at his shoulder, behind him again. "You need to trust, David. Not for her, but for you."

David's chest heaved as his ribs seemed to close in around his heart. His stomach snapped back to its familiar knot. "It's not fair!"

The voice from behind him quavered. "I know. But your unforgiveness is killing you. It's eating you alive, yet I know you can do it. You can forgive your wife."

David slammed his eyes shut as his whole body shuddered. No, he couldn't do this.

The Baggage Handler's voice was now all

around him. "Your pain was starting to go. Remember how you felt—"

David breathed hard through his nose as the injustice, explosive fuel to a tinder-dry righteous anger, flooded back through him. "I know exactly how I felt. Ripped off. Used."

"But, David—"

The fuel ignited and rage swallowed him whole. With a primal scream, six months of pain and hurt surged through him. He dropped the polo shirt and photo and pounded his fists on the mirror, which shattered into a spiderweb of destruction. He pounded the mirror again, and it exploded into a billowing cloud of shards and glass dust. David pummeled the mirror again and again, each hammerblow driven by a guttural scream. He slumped to his knees as the sobs racked his body, his fists still stuck to the mirror.

The Baggage Handler's voice was now a whisper. "Oh, David. It looks like you've made a choice."

David dragged himself to his feet, spun in a fury, and faced the Baggage Handler with fiery, narrowed eyes. "Yes, I have. Now, let me out of here!"

The Baggage Handler bit a quivering lip. "Even if it means carrying this baggage around with you for the rest of your life?"

David panted through clenched teeth, and his

chest heaved in defiance. "Yep. I didn't notice it was there before."

"I don't think I can do much more for you this time." The Baggage Handler brushed aside the shards of glass and picked up the polo shirt and photo. He placed them into the suitcase and zipped it up.

David moved to lift his baggage, wary of the last time he'd tried to lift it. "So now I can leave?"

The Baggage Handler stood back with a sweep of his arm. "You've made your choice, so you've fulfilled your contract. For now." Tears filmed his blue eyes before they trickled their way down his cheeks. "My hope is that you will find your way back here."

David breathed his white-hot rage, savoring the power. It might come in handy for the board presentation. "There's no way I'll be coming back."

The Baggage Handler brushed away the tears. "I hope you will, David. You need to."

David's chest heaved as he lunged for the suitcase and lifted it. This time there was no resistance, just weight. "Whoever you are, whatever you are, it's been fun. But I've got to get back on track to save my career."

The Baggage Handler stepped back and opened the door. "The offer is always there. You know where to find me. You found me this time."

"Yeah, whatever." David peered around the doorframe, expecting to see the corridor disappearing into infinity as it had before. Instead, there was a large black door in front of him, open to the street.

27

Gillian's heart fluttered as she looked deep into the eyes of the stranger in the mirror.

She was . . . beautiful? Sparkling hazel eyes not surrounded with the dark circles she expected. Blond hair that was tidy and neat in defiance of an early-morning plane trip. She took in her full reflection. Her blouse was crisp and not creased, her dress pants were fresh and not crumpled, and her thighs weren't the massive legs of mutton she'd been convinced they were.

The Baggage Handler stood behind her, tears pricking his eyes. "This is how the rest of the world views you. It would be great if you could see what we all see."

Gillian's breath deserted her as she raised a hand and wiggled fingers she'd always seen as age ravaged and chubby. Her reflection's slender fingers did the same. "I had no idea."

"I think in a way you didn't want to allow yourself to have an idea."

The stranger in the mirror stared back. A stranger who reminded her of her younger self, before time, three boys, and comfort chocolate exacted a heavy toll. The heaviness Gillian constantly needed to sigh away was gone. She felt . . . okay. Good about herself, even.

Her reflection looked over Gillian's left shoulder, and then her right. Gillian's mouth fell open, and then her reflection caught her gaze and winked before looking down at the floor.

Wisps of fog billowed around the feet of her reflection. Gillian looked down at her own feet. Nothing. Back in the mirror, white-marble-and-dark-gray clouds billowed to fill the reflection of the waiting room, a mesmerizing wave of drifting, rolling smoke.

Gillian's heart skipped a beat at the hint of movement behind her reflection. Ghosted figures swept from one side of the mirror to the other, flying through the gray.

Gillian's reflection looked to one side as one ghosted figure flew in and settled next to her. The outline of a person appeared at her side, a head taller than her, at a height both comfortable and recognizable. The cloud pushed back as waves of color swept through the outline, a shimmering kaleidoscope that filled in the figure from the edges. A belt appeared around the figure's waist, similar to a belt she'd picked up from her bedroom floor a thousand times before. She saw light-brown chinos and a blue polo shirt, embroidered with a company logo on the chest. She'd washed shirts just like that one a thousand times.

Features materialized—kind blue eyes, brown, curly hair thinning at the top, and a goofy smile that could both infuriate her and melt her heart. The face of her husband.

Rick looked down at her reflection, that goofy smile plastered all over his face. Her reflection returned his loving gaze.

Gillian smiled at the mirror as her reflection reached for Rick's hand.

To the left of her reflection, the smoke parted as three smaller figures ghosted in, one taller, two the same size. Waves of kaleidoscopic color swept back and forth across their figures as details filled in. Bike helmets and skinned knees. Mismatched socks and holey basketball shoes. Her boys. They looked up at their mother's reflection with admiration, love burning in their eyes. Tyson grabbed her reflection's hand and squeezed it.

That broke the dam wall of Gillian's emotions, and the tears started.

"What—"

The Baggage Handler's voice appeared behind her, above her, all around her.

"Watch."

Rick took one step back and brought his hands together in a soft clap. Her boys joined in the applause for their mother. Their enthusiasm rose to a crescendo, the four men in her life cheering and whooping. Her reflection basked in the appreciation and stood tall.

The tears cascaded down Gillian's cheeks as

her family acknowledged her for who she was in this scene of love . . . and of something elusive. Her reflection showed her something that made her feel . . .

Gillian looked over her shoulder. Her family wasn't there, but the Baggage Handler was. His tears fell without shame as he joined in the applause and nodded toward the mirror.

A blinding white light shone out of the mirror, and Gillian shielded her eyes as tendrils of golden light sprung from the mirror and reached out to her. She raised a hand, and the tendrils wrapped around her fingers. Pulsing. Stroking. Warm. Loving. And something else.

Accepting.

More tendrils of light swept toward her, stroking her cheek and her hair and wrapping her in a warm embrace. The tears flowed down her face as she breathed deep to capture this affirmation and hold it within her.

In the mirror, Rick stepped forward and wrapped an arm around her reflection. He turned to Gillian and spoke. She didn't hear his words as much as feel their resonance deep within her.

"Gillian, you're good enough as you are."

With his words, the tendrils released her and retreated into the mirror. The bright light pulsing from the mirror dimmed.

The gray smoke drifted back across the mirror as the figures dematerialized. With a final squeeze of her reflection's hand from Tyson, the boys faded away. Rick leaned forward and kissed her reflection's cheek, and then the color drained from him as well. Her family was gone. Then, in an instant, the cloud dissipated, and Gillian stood staring at her own reflection, radiating warmth and contentment as if she'd stepped out of a warm bath.

Gillian looked down at herself. What she saw in the mirror was a true reflection of who she was.

She wiped away the tears with the back of her hand and turned on her heel. She faced this young man, who was also wiping away the emotion. "Who are you?"

He stood to attention and tipped his cap, curly, black hair springing free across his forehead. "I'm the Baggage Handler. Now, let me show you the way out."

28

Michael's eyes followed the Baggage Handler's finger to his open suitcase. What else was in there apart from his running spikes and design portfolio?

Sitting on top of the familiar chocolate brown of his design portfolio was one final certificate. A piece of paper not badged by Serviceton High School. A piece of paper that looked familiar. An artistic merit certificate with his name emblazed on it. Pride from another time coursed through him—until he saw the comment scrawled across the bottom in a heavy black hand.

Not good enough.

Michael had never seen that. Each of his certificates was placed in a folder that took pride of place on his bedroom bookshelf, next to his design portfolio. None of them were ever critiqued. They couldn't have been. No one ever saw them. But something about the handwriting was familiar. Very familiar.

"Where did this come from?"

The Baggage Handler sat back on the sofa, sadness in his eyes. "That's been in your baggage for a very long time."

Michael stared hard at the thick, heavy hand

of the black ink at the bottom of the paper. His memory stirred.

"Whose handwriting is that?"

The Baggage Handler nodded. "I think you know, Michael."

A single memory stepped forward, captioned by that thick, chunky writing: the yard work to-do list for the weekend, every weekend since he was five.

The Baggage Handler's voice was soft and conspiratorial. "That one is the hardest."

Is that it? One piece of paper? Easy. I'll hand it over and try to find a way to get back to the university.

Michael reached into his suitcase, but his hand was met by an invisible guardian—a magnetic wall his fingers couldn't break through. He pulled out his hand and looked at the Baggage Handler, who nodded in encouragement.

Michael again reached out. First his thumb trembled, and then his fingers joined in the tremor. His hand was swamped by a heavy gravity, and the tension jolted up his arm as it pushed toward the paper. He withdrew it and sat back on his haunches.

The Baggage Handler squatted next to him, a comforting hand on his shoulder. "Keep going."

Michael tried again, his fingers curling as he pushed back against the repulsion. His arm shook, and he summoned every ounce of energy he had. His fingers spasmed, and then, with a pop and a jolt, his hand pushed through and grasped the last remaining certificate. The emotions swelled within him, clamoring up inside him, choking his breath. Unbidden, two tears ran down his cheeks and dropped onto the paper, blurring the heavy handwritten comment. He took a deep breath in an unsuccessful fight to force down these emotions that had blindsided him.

"Here." The Baggage Handler held out Michael's design portfolio in one hand and an open hand for the artistic merit certificate.

Michael grasped his design portfolio as he held out the paper for the Baggage Handler to take. The second half of the equation didn't happen. Michael's fingers did not—would not—let go. He willed them to release their grip, but they wouldn't cooperate. A panic crested within him. "What's going on? I can't let it go."

"That's not unusual."

"Why? I'm just letting go of a piece of paper."

The Baggage Handler shook his head. "You're letting go of far more than that. Many people find it hard."

"Why is it so hard?"

"Because you have been defined by this." The Baggage Handler fixed a gaze on him with clouded blue eyes, a look approaching wistfulness. "What did you say when I said you probably would have missed out on the scholarship anyway?"

Michael racked his brain, but nothing was there.

"Exactly. You said nothing. No protest, no standing up for yourself and your talents. No disagreement. It was as if deep down you agreed with what I was saying."

Maybe I did. "You might be right."

"Your baggage defines you, Michael. Your dad has told you you're no good for years, and that has shaped you."

The Baggage Handler jiggled the design portfolio. "This is great. And while you may have missed this opportunity today, that won't be the only chance you'll have to impress people with your art. But if you leave today without letting go, well . . ."

More tears trickled down Michael's cheeks. He jammed his eyes shut and willed his fingers to open, but they had his certificate in an iron grip.

"You are a talented artist," the Baggage Handler said.

The tears still flowed as Michael was bathed in affirmation.

The Baggage Handler nodded toward the certificate. "So what do you say?"

Michael again willed his fingers to let go. The thick, condemning black handwriting at the foot of the page blurred as sobs racked Michael's body. The paper quivered in his hand, and years of rejection bubbled to the surface and found their way out. Finally.

Minutes passed, although it could have been hours. He first felt a flicker in his index finger—the tiniest muscle spasm. *I have to let go.* Another flicker, this time larger. *I have to let go.* His fingers complied and snapped open. At that moment, more than a weight lifted off Michael's shoulders. He was weightless, as if gravity no longer applied to him. He was no longer bound by the force that had kept him low for so long.

Michael clutched the design portfolio to his chest.

The Baggage Handler wiped tears away with the back of his hand. "Congratulations! You've done far more than most people ever do. You're an artist, Michael."

Those words wrapped Michael in what felt like a warm blanket. It was more than comfortable, it was . . . right. He *was* an artist.

Then, on cue, the doubts shuffled their way back to the surface and smothered him in a familiar cloak of discomfort. The faint echo of his father's voice filled the corners of his mind, and his eyes dropped to the carpet.

The Baggage Handler sidled up and put an arm around him. "Come with me." He ushered Michael to the full-length mirror.

Michael jelly-legged his way to this mirror,

feeling somewhat foolish but still light-headed from the exchange with this strange guy and whatever had just happened.

"What do you see, Michael?"

Michael looked at the Baggage Handler's reflection standing next to his. "Me. Why?"

An edge of excitement crept into the Baggage Handler's voice. "I didn't ask *who* you see; I asked *what* you see."

Michael stared hard at the Baggage Handler's reflection. He juggled the design portfolio and shifted it from one hand to the other. He opened it, tracing his fingers along the lines of artwork that had burned into his memory.

Then the words came, first to his mind, and then, unusually, they burst from his mouth. "An artist."

The Baggage Handler's voice now sounded like it was miles away. "What do you see, Michael?"

Michael's voice strengthened as his confidence in his newfound identity grew. "I see an artist."

His eyes flicked to the mirror, and the Baggage Handler's reflection was gone. The surface of the mirror was now shimmering, liquid mercury.

A figure emerged through the liquid and stood tall in the center of the mirror. It was a man in his late thirties, goateed and dressed in the familiar, manic crisscross of a T-shirt designed by Jackson Pollock. Small circular glasses hid eyes he'd seen a thousand times.

His eyes.

How could that be? This man was at least twenty years older than him.

The Baggage Handler's voice came from behind him. Above him. Everywhere. "What do you see?"

Michael's voice was strong, powerful. Believing. "I see an artist."

The figure in the mirror smiled, and then turned away. The background behind him filled in to reveal an expansive room, spotlights bouncing from white walls onto polished black concrete. Sketches held in tiny black frames dotted each wall, taking pride of place in the glare of the spotlights.

Michael knew this room—the long timber lines of the floor, the sheer white of the wall, the banks of sweeping spotlights—even though he had been there just once. It was the Museum of Modern Art in New York City, the scene of his wildest dreams.

The figure in the mirror moved toward the sketches, and people appeared to his left and right, champagne glasses in hand. They patted him on the back and crowded around him for selfies.

Michael smiled at the scene and squinted hard at the tiny frames. He recognized the sketch of his first girlfriend and his self-portrait. And the sketch of his mother, his first attempt at art. His art teacher had said it unveiled a talent he should pursue.

On the far wall of the museum, a banner unfurled from the ceiling: Michael Downer, the Early Years. His future self stood between his sketches, a broad smile on his face as photographers snapped his picture. He had something Michael yearned to have.

Purpose.

Confidence.

Contentment.

The scene in the mirror flickered, and then faded. Michael reached out an instinctive hand to prolong the vision, but soon the mirror's surface was back to liquid mercury.

The Baggage Handler's voice appeared at his shoulder. "Your future. The one you'll have if you accept who you are and chase a dream that's yours."

Michael's head swam as his mind tried to process everything. He was going to be an artist. It would be all right. He looked at the mirror. His own reflection was back, still clutching the design portfolio to his chest.

The Baggage Handler stepped forward next to him. "That's great to see."

"What?"

"You didn't sigh. You've been sighing since you got here."

"That's my future?"

"It is if you accept who you are."

Michael nodded as a peace washed over him. He would become an artist. Maybe not yet since he had missed his scholarship interview, but it would come. "How do I get out of here?"

The Baggage Handler pulled his cell phone from his pocket. "I'll call you a cab." He whistled while the phone rang, and he got to the chorus of the song that had been buzzing around Michael's head since he first heard it. He couldn't help but sing along. "R-E-S-P-E-C-T." He laughed as he shook his head. He should have known that tune—he had heard it coming out of the kitchen enough times while his mother baked.

Michael zipped up his suitcase and, still unsure, tested it to make sure he could pick it up. He could, with ease.

"The cab is on its way; it's booked in your name." The Baggage Handler extended a hand. "It's been great to meet you, Michael. I'm so glad we had the chance."

Michael gave him a broad smile. "Now, what about this opportunity that's just around the corner?"

The Baggage Handler returned Michael's smile and winked. "You'll see."

29

David blinked in the harsh glare of the bright sunshine as the wall of heat extracted beads of sweat from his forehead. He surveyed the street and walked toward the intersection, hoping to find a cab.

A solitary car approached in the distance. It was a taxi, which, based on the abandoned streets, David thought must be lost. A stroke of luck. He plopped his suitcase on the sidewalk and hailed the cab.

The driver slowed, and the passenger window lowered. "Michael Downer? I've been booked for a Michael Downer."

David threw a furtive glance down the street as familiar confidence surged through him. He could be a Michael for the next ten minutes. "Um, yeah, that's me." He started to open the door, but the driver had noticed the hesitation, and his eyes narrowed. "Really? You got some ID, pal?"

David's shoulders slumped. Beaten. The driver reached over and pulled the door shut, and then he drove away.

He trudged down the street, this strange white building at his shoulder the whole way. His suitcase dragged on his arm. His phone reconnected with the world and his thumb searched for Julian's number. How was he going to describe all this to his boss? Putting it down to stress would make the whole thing worse. But the airline would get the blame, and he would sue the pants off them if he lost his job. His stomach grumbled, desperate for antacid relief.

His phone buzzed. A text message. From Sharon.

When you get back, we need to talk.

David dismissed her text with a flick of his thumb and savored the feeling of power that coursed through him. *We'll talk, all right, and I've got a few choice things to say.* He smirked at the building that had kept him captive for hours. *Deal with baggage. Whatever. I knew I was right.* Before he could punch Julian's number, his phone rang. Sharon. Self-satisfaction flowed through him as he toyed with shunting her to voice mail. But with a sense of superiority, he took the call.

"What?"

Breathy sobbing burst from the phone.

It wasn't Sharon.

"Daddy, Daddy . . ."

Caitlin.

David shielded his eyes from the burning sun as he looked left and right for a taxi.

"Caitie, what's going on?" His heart thumped hard in his chest. He clutched at it as he sat on his suitcase, the sweat running in rivulets down his back.

His daughter cried and cried, her words choked back by sobs.

"Caitie, Daddy's here. Daddy's here. Just take a deep breath and tell me what's going on." *Where's Sharon?*

Caitlin sniffed back the tears, and each of her tiny breaths sucked the joy from his heart.

"Daddy, Mommy's just packed all the suitcases, and there's a van in the driveway."

David's heart seemed to sink into his stomach, now stewing in a broiling wash of acid. A hot wind whipped through the chain-link fence and extracted another wave of sweat.

"She says we're going to stay at Grandma's for a while. Are we still going to see the princesses?"

30

Michael reached for his wallet, and a sinking realization hit him. He didn't have quite enough money for both another twenty-two-dollar ride and another cab back to the airport. But he should go back to the university and give Coach Crosswell some kind of explanation. He owed him that.

The usual feelings of inadequacy again stepped forward, but they were different. Without power. He could *do* this.

The Baggage Handler put out a hand to stop him. "That's okay. I've already paid for it."

Michael pushed the hand aside and rushed forward to envelop the Baggage Handler in a hug. "Thank you so much." As he squeezed, the last of his anxiety and worthlessness flowed from him. He slapped the Baggage Handler on the shoulder.

"My pleasure." The Baggage Handler tipped his cap. "That's what I'm here for." He led Michael back to the reception area and the door to the street.

A horn tooted outside, announcing the taxi's arrival.

Michael headed out, the Baggage Handler in tow.

The driver's side window rolled down, revealing a young man in an open-necked shirt and tidy haircut. Not the driver who had brought him here. Thank goodness for that.

"Michael Downer?"

Michael nodded, jumped into the taxi, and told the driver where he needed to go. Michael looked out the back window as the cab pulled away. The Baggage Handler simply smiled and tipped his cap.

What was this new opportunity? It had to be another chance to run for Coach. Maybe a spot had opened in his busy schedule. That had to be it.

The heavy weight he'd become used to shouldering again fought its way back. If the opportunity wasn't running for Coach, he'd have to face Dad's ire and disappointment, and the usual dread loomed over him as another frantic thought flitted through his mind. He was going to be an artist, but how would he get there? His father would never support his college tuition in the arts; he'd made that crystal clear for as long as Michael could hold a pencil.

Michael's cell phone flickered into service and R2-D2 was back. A voice message.

Coach?

No.

"Michael, Robyn Tonkin from the art school at Clarendon University. Your art teacher sent some samples of your work to me, and I'm impressed. I understand you're here at CU to talk to the athletics program, but I would love to meet with you and talk about opportunities here at the art school, including a scholarship that might interest you. Would you mind giving me a call?"

Emotion welled up in Michael as his great opportunity appeared in front of him. His heart seemed to swell in his chest, and he clutched his portfolio tighter.

He could *do* this.

Michael looked out of the back window. The shrinking figure of the Baggage Handler simply tipped his hat again.

31

Gillian stood blinking on the street as her eyes adjusted to the bright sunlight. She was nearly floating, and she couldn't help but smile. Becky would be angry with her for taking her time dealing with her baggage, but that was okay. What she'd experienced was worth the apology she would have to make.

Wheeling her suitcase behind her, she crossed the street to where Becky was waiting. The Audi looked a little dirtier than before.

Gillian threw her suitcase into the back and then jumped into the passenger seat. "I'm so sorry it's taken this long." She braced herself for Becky's onslaught.

Becky looked up from her phone. "What are you talking about? You've been gone five minutes. I think that's pretty good. We're almost back on schedule."

Gillian glanced at the cracked dial of the clock on the Audi's dashboard. Becky wasn't kidding. How could it have been just five minutes? She smiled to herself as she pulled down the car's visor and looked at herself in the mirror. Her reflection was the same as she'd last seen it in the baggage depot. The bags under her eyes weren't as pronounced, and now there was a sparkle in her eyes.

Becky started down the street as Gillian whistled that song that was so familiar. Then lyrics that had eluded her burst from her lips: "You're beautiful / you're beautiful, it's true." Gillian chuckled. So *that's* what he was whistling.

As she smiled out the front window, from the corner of her eye she saw Becky look at her. "You seem to have perked up a lot. You got your baggage sorted out, then?"

"More than you'll ever know." Gillian turned to her sister and tried again to connect. "When will I get to catch up with Brent?"

The Audi slowed ever so slightly, and Becky's gaze lingered for too long in the rearview mirror.

Gillian decided to persist. It was an important question to ask. "It would be good to know how he's doing."

Becky was silent, which was new in itself. Gillian studied her sister, the superhero who needed the cape. The crow's-feet around Becky's eyes crinkled as tears welled.

"If we're going to catch up over lunch, Becky, it would be good to know how you're *really* doing. It's been too long since we've really talked, you know, properly."

Her sister's knuckles whitened on the steering wheel before she choked back a sigh. "Did I tell you Jessica's wedding dress is based on a design from that Hollywood wedding TV show . . ."

Gillian looked back at the white building as it

disappeared into the side mirror. A lone figure stood outside it, and she could just make him out in the distance as they drove away. He was doffing his navy-blue cap.

—Epilogue—

The Baggage Handler leaned on his shiny silver baggage cart in the deserted baggage claim area of the airport. The carousels were quiet.

A low rumble in the distance announced another fleet of aircraft bringing more passengers who needed help with their baggage. He smiled as the screens flickered into life and directed a tsunami of travelers his way.

Young backpackers, carefree and not beholden to any clock or calendar.

Young mothers with babes in arms, relieved at escaping from the microscope of a plane full of passengers.

Kids running ahead of tired parents who had given up their demands to slow down.

Retirees on vacations they'd worked a lifetime to earn.

Businessmen on the run to or from the machinations of a deal.

They all headed in his direction.

Some of the travelers struggled with backpacks and jam-packed carry-on baggage as if the weight was too much to carry. Some hurried as if they were racing Father Time himself. Some of them dawdled as if picking up their baggage would start a journey they didn't want to begin.

The Baggage Handler smiled and tipped his cap toward the incoming crowd. He spun the cart with effortless ease and headed toward them, a whistle on his lips.

—A Note from the Author—

Hi, friend. Thanks for reading *The Baggage Handler*. I appreciate the time you've taken to not only read but digest a story I've had a lot of fun writing.

We all have baggage. Some of it we packed ourselves and willingly carry. Some was packed for us, and we carry it out of favor or responsibility. And some was jammed in there without our knowing.

But no matter how it got there, we still feel its weight.

The following questions aren't designed to be homework, nor are they designed to be one of those study group worksheets you diligently work through from top to bottom. They are designed to start your own thought processes, conversations, or discussions about baggage—or any other issues raised.

How do you respond to the issue of your baggage, how it got there, and how you're carrying it?

If it helps, I'll start whistling a tune that's familiar yet somehow elusive.

Regards,
David

—Some Questions for You—

Chapters 1–7

- Do you know people who show signs of carrying baggage? What are those signs?
- Do you identify with any of the characters in this story? If so, which character do you identify with the most?
- Do you see other people in your life in these characters? (If so, lend them this book.)
- Do you know of people like Becky? What impact do they have on you?
- If Michael could have impressed the coach, how do you think he would have fared?
- Do you think David's mantra of remembering happier times is enough to help him deal with his issues? Should it be?
- What is Gillian's real baggage?

Chapters 8–14

- Do you see any link between David's branch being considered for closing and David's baggage?
- What do you believe the Baggage Services building is?
- Why do you think the entry points to Baggage Services are different for each of the three characters?

- Do you think there's significance in Gillian's ability to easily find the entrance while the other two characters have to hunt for it?

Chapters 15–20
- If you were to go to Baggage Services, what do you think your waiting room would look like?
- What do you think is the general theme of Michael's waiting room?
- Why do you think Gillian's waiting room seemed perfect?
- What do you think is the significance of the rust color on the cloth the Baggage Handler used to clean Gillian's glasses?
- If you consider David's waiting room, what role do you think the alarm clock plays? Do you have a ticking clock in your life?
- What do you think is the significance of David's encounter in the corridor?

Chapters 21–27
- Do you think it's fair that David is carrying baggage even though his wife was the one who broke her marriage vows? Why or why not?
- Why do you think David can't simply tear up his baggage and throw it away?
- What do you think is the impact of refusing

to forgive others? Do you know people who simply refuse to forgive others who have hurt them? How is that working for them?

- At what stage of each encounter does the Baggage Handler look at David, Gillian, and Michael with a look approaching wistfulness? What do you think that look means?
- Michael's baggage was packed by his father. Do you think that's fair? Why or why not?
- How do others place items into your baggage? Is that fair?

Chapters 28–31

- Why do you think it's important for David to forgive his wife instead of just moving on after leaving his baggage behind?
- What significance do you think is in each character needing to look into a mirror before being allowed to move on from Baggage Services?
- Why do you think Gillian has so much trouble doing that? Would you?
- Why do you think Michael finds it hard to let go of his certificate?
- What do you think it is about baggage that defines us?
- Do you think it's possible to live life without any baggage?
- Why do you think people find it difficult to deal with issues in their lives?

- What was the impact of Gillian comparing herself to everyone in her life?
- In what distorted ways do you—or those around you—see yourself? What mirror do you use?

—Acknowledgments—

To God: thank you for sending this idea, for the ability to do it justice, and for helping me make time in a crowded schedule to put it on the page.

To my family: Nicky, Cameron, Daniella, and Emily, thank you for your patience in allowing me to chase this idea, and to my parents, thank you for your unwavering support.

To my publishing team at Thomas Nelson: Becky Monds, my editorial director, thank you for wanting to see this story on the shelves almost as much as I did; Paul Fisher and his team, thanks for your willingness to kick ideas around; and Amanda Bostic and the rest of the team, thank you for the great work you do in bringing great stories to life.

To my supporters: James L. Rubart, thanks for your guidance, connections, and unbridled enthusiasm; Steve Laube, thanks for taking a chance with a story that was different; and the Fulwood family, thank you for your ideas and friendship.

To my global colleagues: Karen Sargent, Tisha Martin, Sarah Nuss, Ian Acheson, and Jebraun Clifford, thank you for your support over great distance—among the support of many, many others.

To the counselors I've spoken with and worked with: thanks for your insights and your passion for helping people be the best people they can be.

All characters in this work are fictitious. Resemblance to real persons, living or dead, is purely coincidental, although based on my forty-odd years of dealing with people.

No baggage was harmed in the writing of this story, although it was dealt with—as it should be.

Center Point Large Print
600 Brooks Road / PO Box 1
Thorndike, ME 04986-0001 USA

(207) 568-3717

US & Canada:
1 800 929-9108
www.centerpointlargeprint.com